The Case Files Of Martin Brothers

Abhigyan Sarma

Invincible Publishers

First published in India in 2017 by Invincible Publishers

ISBN: 978-93-86148-57-5

Invincible Publishers
G - 120, Sushant Lok III, Sector 57, Gurgaon-122002

Opposite Kasturba Ashram, Radaur Distt Yamuna Nagar, Haryana- 135133

Digitally Printed at Replika Press Pvt. Ltd.

Dedication –

Dedicated to my late father, Mr. Tapan Mohan Sarma, who passed away in March 2010. We miss you, Dad.

Contents

Acknowledgment

❄ ❄ ❄

A writer can just write a story. However, even that is not possible without support from the family. Hence, I would like to start by thanking my family - my mother and my brother, who have always supported me in my decision to publish a book. Without their love and constant support this wouldn't have been possible. Thank you for all that you have given and for helping me grow as a person.

Next, I would like to thank the entire team of Invincible Publishers in making my dream come true. Ajay Setia, who was always there to guide me in the publishing process, to which I am so new. He was the first person I talked to from the entire team and I must say that he along with the others treated my book like their own. I also thank my editor, Malvika Solanki, without who, the story wouldn't have been half as readable as it is now. Her suggestions and unwavering support helped in making this story come alive and Sneha Agarwal for the splendid book cover. I also thank the rest of the team of Invincible Publishers. Without who, my story would have just remained a story on my laptop.

Finally, I would like to thank all the readers who purchased this book. Your support is what I seek ultimately, and your feedback and productive criticism is what will motivate me to present the next editions of the series. I still need all the help and inspiration I can get and hence would appreciate your continued support.

Well, that just about covers it all.

Let's start off the series now with 'All That Glitters...'

Preface

* * *

Young boys often try to play detective when they are fascinated by them courtesy to the various books they read and movies they watch. But most of them literally just 'play' detective and are seldom serious. However, I had the privilege to know three young boys who actually took the term 'detective' seriously. It looked as if they had it in their blood. I had met them in Fischerberg City when I had gone there to pursue my higher education. I stayed there for two years and in that time, got to know John, Joe and Jeff Martin quite well as they lived in the same street as mine. They were commonly called 'the three Js' and had become quite popular in the city. They solved a number of cases including some where the Police was completely baffled. It all started when they retrieved a stolen necklace that belonged to a museum and continued with their brave deeds to help the cops nab some poachers. I was fortunate enough to befriend them and also help them in a few of the cases. We would often spend our free time together and when there was nothing else to do, the three Js would tell me of their adventures. I didn't feel that I should keep the stories that I heard from them all to myself. Hence, I thought of penning them down so that the entire world could read about their heroism and come to know about their cases. I am starting off the series with a case where they embark on a treasure hunt. Everyone loves treasure hunt and I felt this would be the best case to start the series with.

1
The Visitor

* * *

"The lost treasure of the ship 'Longest Yard' that had drowned 80 years back has been discovered in the Atlantic..." the voice from the news channel echoed.

"Gosh! I had thought all the treasure had been discovered already," exclaimed Jeff Martin, the 19-year-old averagely built, college going boy lying on the couch in the Martins' Residence on 12th Sandy Street, Yorkville, Fischerberg City. An adventurous happy-go-lucky youth, Jeff, 5' 9", was an outdoor lover with a good sense of all the requisites required for an outdoor activity, be it camping or trekking. He could guess the direction without a compass more often than not by reading the position of the stars, the moon and certainly, the sun.

"Same here, man! This is quite a discovery," John replied.

John Martin, Jeff's cousin, was a 21-year-old, 5'11", college student at the same college as Jeff, that is, Green Hills Academy, was another averagely built chap with a good craze for working out. Apart from going to the gym, he loved researching on current affairs and working out with the computer trying out and learning various programming languages. He was very much the computer geek and the athlete in the group.

John's younger brother Joe, who also went to Green Hills Academy, at 19 years of age, was another fine averagely built guy with a good interest in mysteries and detective stories. At 5'10", he was the one who took the boys into the line of solving some of the very important mysteries and crime in Fischerberg City. Although quite lazy, his laziness stood no chance against his love for camping and trekking himself.

The boys, popularly known as 'the three Js' had solved a few crimes including one where they caught some poachers and another where they caught the thieves of a gold necklace that was stolen from a museum. The few cases had given them a little fame around the city and the academy did not waste any time in rewarding them for the bravery.

They now relaxed at the Martins' Residence which belonged to John and Joe's family in the lazy afternoon. Summer vacations had just started and their parents had gone out for shopping and to watch a movie. The three finding themselves nothing to do had switched on the T.V and were surfing through the channels when they struck upon the news of the newly discovered treasure.

"Wish we too could get a chance to go on a treasure hunt," sighed Joe too bored.

"I heard there's a treasure hunt competition coming up in a few days as a part of the Annual Fest of the Youth Club of Yorkville," Jeff said remembering what he had heard from a college friend of his "I guess, we should give it a try."

"Agree," Joe replied, "We anyway have nothing better to do throughout the vacations."

"I guess I will take up some courses on one or two programming languages to spend my vacations," John informed.

"Come on, bro," Joe sighed "You can't study during vacations."

"No use telling John that," Jeff added amid a smile from John.

"You're right," Joe submitted "Anyway, do you know where we need to register for the treasure hunt you told us about?"

"No, I will have to ask him," Jeff replied, "I will do that once I go home."

"I'll tell you what," John suggested, "Why don't we play the new pack of cards we bought last week, Joe?"

"Good idea," Joe agreed as Jeff nodded.

Joe went upstairs to their room to fetch the new playing cards. Martins' Residence was a two story building with a hall at the front. It was accompanied by the dining hall cum counter kitchen towards one side and a bedroom towards the other side which belonged to the boys' parents. Upstairs, one room belonged to the brothers while another room was utilized as a guest room. The hall where the boys were seated comprised of a Cabriole sofa set and an LCD T.V hanging at the wall in front of it. A sisal carpet in the center of the sofas with an Asian center table placed on it gave the hall an overall modern look.

The boys played the new cards throughout the afternoon. After a couple of hours, though, they got bored of playing. When college was on, the boys longed for a vacation. Now that vacations had started, the boys longed for college to reopen. After playing the pack of cards for some time, Jeff informed that his mother, who happened to be John and Joe's aunt, had given him some chores to do and hence, he bid farewell to the boys for the evening.

"It's only 4," Joe sighed after Jeff had left "Mom and

Dad would be back only by dinner time."

"I know," John replied "I am going upstairs. I want to do some research on how many more treasures are there in the world undiscovered."

"I don't think there are any left," Joe guessed "Anyway, I will read the new novel I had purchased last week."

After about a couple of hours, the doorbell rang at the Martins' Residence.

"Mom and Dad must be back," John said.

"So soon?" Joe asked as he got down from his bed, keeping aside his novel.

He rushed downstairs and opened the door to be greeted by a husky man who seemed to be in his late fifties. He wore a red full sleeve shirt and black trousers. A brown cowboy hat on his head gave him a look which Joe had only seen in movies.

"Hello," the man greeted in a rather strong voice "I am Jean Bucks. Are you one of the Martin Brothers?"

"Yes," Joe replied still trying to figure out who the person was "I am Joe Martin."

"Glad to meet you then," the man said, "I have come here asking for help."

"Uh ok. But what kind of help?"

With a figure as big as a giant and looking as healthy and strong as a gym trainer, it amused Joe that he needed their help. He seemed to be the kind of person that could help anyone in the world. Any damsel in distress would love to have someone like him to help and protect her.

"It ain't something to be discussed outside," Mr. Bucks said sporting a grin which made Joe try to remember even harder if he had seen this man before.

"Oh well, then do come in," Joe offered still trying to think.

As he led the man to the hall closing the main door

behind him, John arrived downstairs.

"Please sit," Joe said making himself comfortable on the couch with John.

Mr. Jean Bucks sat down on a single sofa and took off his hat. He seemed to have come straight out of some movie.

Joe had already told John the man's name by now and both of them waited in silence for the man to speak.

"You must be John," the man finally asked.

"Yes, Joe's elder brother," John replied.

"Well, I know you guys are thinking who I am and why I am here, so let me introduce myself. I am Jean Bucks, as you already know by now, and I live in the outskirts of the city, on the highway leading to Portville Town, in St. Bryan's. I work at Binco's Rubber factory in the Industrial area and I earn a pretty good amount of money which is enough to support me. I was never married, so I have no children. Hence, I stay all alone at my family heirloom house which belonged to my Great-Great Grandfather. Now let me tell you why I am here."

"We are all ears," John said eager to know the purpose of the man's visit.

"But before that, I would like to know if there's anyone else in the house," asked Mr. Bucks.

"No," John replied suspecting something "Our parents have gone out. But I would like to call Jeff over. Seems like you've got a case for us."

"Correct guess, child," Mr. Bucks replied with a gleam on his face. "Go on, call your cousin. I have heard of him as well."

John got up from the couch to make the phone call to the Martin's Abode - Jeff's residence.

"Hello! Jeff here."

"Hey Jeff, John here."

"Hi, John! Sorry, I forgot to ask about the

registration for the treasure hunt competition. I will call him right now and let you know."

"Leave it, Jeff. Just hurry up and come over to our home. There's a man here who has a case for us."

"Great! Coming right over.

2

A Bit of History and Some Ears

* * *

Within five minutes, Jeff arrived who lived just round the corner. The distance was barely a few minutes' walk. The brothers introduced their cousin to the man and the three Js sat on the couch facing the man on the single sofa.

"I hope you guys know about the World War 1?" Mr. Bucks asked in a rather husky voice to which the boys nodded.

"Well, this is a story about Romania," Jean Bucks continued "During the World War 1, the Romanian king had signed a pact with the German-led Triple Alliance in 1883. However, Romania delayed its decision to enter the war until 1916 as they had other more pressing concerns. One of that was the safe keeping of the national treasure. Under King Carol the first, who was named the ruling Prince in 1866, the country enjoyed an era of relative stability and prosperity. The nation had vast resources of treasure in the form of Gold, Jewelries, Arts and Painting and other cultural riches. However, after the King died in 1914, the new leaders realized that whether the Germans invaded or were invited in, the nation's treasures were in the danger of being seized. Romania back then wasn't a strong nation and it sure wasn't capable enough of safe keeping its treasures from the mighty German forces."

Jean Bucks paused for a moment to see if the boys were following. They were.

"Now," Mr. Bucks resumed "Germany controlled most of Central Europe, so there was no way the Romanians could send the treasure to the United States or the United Kingdom for safe keeping. The German forces could intercept it and seize all of it. So the Romanians considered Denmark and Sweden next, but German submarines ruled the North Sea. So with no other choice left, the Romanian leaders made a treaty with Russia, which was USSR back then. The Red Army would safeguard the treasure until after the war."

"How could they trust some other nation with their own treasure?" Joe wondered out loud.

"Exactly," Mr. Bucks replied "So on December 1916, the pact was finally signed with Russia, known as the Romanian-Russian Protocol which guaranteed in great detail, the transport, safekeeping and the return of the Romanian treasure. So the first shipment was sent which comprised of seventeen rail cars of Romanian gold. There were over fifteen hundred crates containing over one hundred tons. That estimated to around three hundred million dollars back then and five billion dollars in today's market."

Mr. Bucks paused to let that sink in.

"Wow! Such a huge amount!" Jeff exclaimed.

"That's not all," Mr. Bucks stated, "Twenty-four additional rail cars were sent in 1917 which comprised of more gold, Jewelry, precious stones and many more riches which were worth around one and a half billion dollars back then."

"That's a lot of money!" John exclaimed.

"It is," Mr. Bucks continued "My Great-Great Grandfather was in Romania back then. He was a merchant who sold things there. I am not sure what things but he spent almost six months every year in Romania. Because of his long stays there, he had made many friends in Romania, one of them, Alexandru Lucas. This man worked for the Government to pack the crates with riches and load them onto the trains that would take them to Moscow. Unknown to the Government, however, he and a few other friends of his took a little of the treasure themselves. Even though the amount was huge for one person, it was so minute when compared to the total worth of the treasure that no one ever noticed. Alexandru got 2 pots of these riches for himself. However, he had no place to keep them and he was scared that if anyone saw his loot, they would hand him over to the Police. So after much thinking, he entrusted his loot with my Great-Great Grandfather and told him to take the loot back with him to the United States. He said that he would himself come to the US after the war ended and take back the riches. My Great-Great Grandfather agreed and started his voyage to return to the United States the next day and never again went back to Romania. The war ended in November 1918 but Alexandru never came to the US. He was probably killed in the war. My Great-Great Grandfather was taken aback by the trust Alexandru had shown with him and so he decided to safeguard the two pots forever. He didn't spend even one gold coin from it and neither did he tell anyone about it. If the Government found out about the treasure, they would take it from him and term it as National Property. So my great Grandfather, after his father's death buried the two pots in the backyard of our house in St. Bryan's."

"That's quite a story," John admitted "But why did you tell us all of this?" he asked still not getting what the case was.

"Yeah," Mr. Bucks replied "The treasure has been there in the backyard of my house all these years. But today morning I saw that someone had dug out one of the pots at night. Someone stole one of the pots!"

"Oh, that's sad," Jeff admitted.

"Who could have done that?" John asked.

"I have no idea," Mr. Bucks replied almost breaking down over the fact that a part of his family treasure was stolen "But I didn't want to report this to the Police because the Police would find the treasure and give it to the Government after taking a part of it. I don't want that to happen. This treasure belongs to us and not to the nation. It belonged to Alexandru, or more say the Romanian Government. But certainly not the US Government."

Mr. Bucks paused to catch his breath and then continued "So I want you guys to find the lost loot."

The boys wondered silently looking at each other.

"I will reward you for it," Mr. Bucks offered.

"It's not about money, Mr. Bucks," John said with a smile "We anyway love adventures. We would love to be on a treasure hunt. We will do all we can to help you."

"Yes, we will," Joe and Jeff agreed in unison.

"Thank you so much, boys," Jean Bucks said gladly with a sign of relief and a flicker of hope on his face.

"Is there anything else we need to know before we start off?" John asked.

"Umm…" Mr. Bucks thought for a moment and then said "I can't think of anything more. Oh yes, please don't tell any of this to anyone. All of this has been a very well maintained secret in our family and I don't want anyone to know about it."

"You can rely on us, Mr. Bucks," Joe assured as the

other two nodded in agreement.

"Well, then that's all. I will take my leave now. But can I get a glass of water before I leave?" Mr. Bucks asked.

"Sure," Joe replied as he got up from the couch and went to the kitchen to get Jean a glass of water.

"Where did you say you live?" Jeff asked Mr. Bucks "We may want to come over and inspect the site ourselves if you're fine with it."

"I am completely fine with it," Mr. Bucks replied.

He produced a visiting card from his wallet and handed it over to Jeff.

"This is my card. It has all the contact details you want. And if you give me a piece of paper, I will write down my address for you."

John took the small pocket notebook from beside the telephone, which was kept there for writing important stuff while talking on the phone. He produced an empty page in the pad and handed it to Mr. Bucks along with a pen.

"Here is your glass of water, Mr. Bucks," Joe said as he re-entered the hall from the kitchen just as Mr. Bucks had finished writing his address.

He took the glass of water, gulped it down quite rapidly and handed the glass back to Joe.

"Thank you so much, guys," he said presently putting the cowboy hat back on top of his head "I will be forever grateful if you are actually successful in helping me."

"We will try our best, sir," John assured as Jean Bucks opened the main door and stepped out onto the porch.

As they bid farewell with word that they would visit his house the next day, a car pulled up into the driveway of the Martins' Residence. It was a black Dodge Duran go, a new six-seater purchased just a few months ago.

"Mom and Dad are here," Joe said as he went over

to the car.

"Hey, Joe," Mr. Oswald Martin greeted his younger son as he got out of the car "Help your mom with the shopping bags, will you?"

Mr. Oswald Martin was the father of John and Joe. He himself was quite athletic and presently in his mid-forties, worked at the Almoor Oil Refinery in the Industrial Area. He was a champion in the Javelin throw and Discus throw in his prime days. However, as age set in, he had developed a small bulgy stomach due to lack of exercise.

His wife, Helena Martin, who was in her early forties was a beautiful averagely built blonde lady with a hobby of cooking new dishes. She served as a Chef in Pigeon's Nest Hotel in Central Fischerberg, before quitting the job just last year to spend more time pursuing her other hobbies like learning the Violin and writing poems. She, however, carried on with her cooking hobby by cooking new and delicious dishes almost every week for her family and also invited Jeff over whenever she did so. She had met Oswald in High School in New York where they married later before Oswald's job brought him to Fischerberg and Helena tagged along with him.

"Hi, Jeff," Mrs. Martin greeted the young boy as soon as she saw him "How are you?"

"I am fine, Aunt Helena," Jeff replied with a nice smile.

"Want to stay over for dinner? I bought some meat and noodles to cook," Mrs. Martin offered.

"No, Aunt Helena," Jeff declined "I should leave now. My Mom must be waiting as I came over in a hurry. Besides, I have to wake up early tomorrow."

He said goodbye to them as John and Joe helped their parents bring the shopping bags inside the house.

"Whew! That's a lot of shopping, Mom," Joe said heaving a sigh of relief once all the bags were inside and they were in the hall.

"I tried to stop your Mom but you know how she acts when she finds herself in the middle of all the shops," Mr. Martin said picking on Helena.

"Come on, Ossie," she replied "Be happy I bought that new Mixer Grinder to replace the old one. Now I can cook new dishes for you guys."

"So what have you guys been doing all this while?" Mr. Oswald asked turning to the boys.

John and Joe took turns to brief their parents about Jean Bucks and the case they had been offered.

"Oh, a treasure hunt!" Helena exclaimed excited once they had finished.

"Yeah," Joe said, "We are excited as well."

"Doesn't seem much danger involved," their father said analyzing the whole scenario "Looks like some petty thieves found out about the treasure and stole it."

"Could be," replied John "But the point is that Mr. Bucks said the treasure had been a well-kept family secret. So how did the thieves come to know about it and why did they steal only one pot?"

None of the other three had any answer to that.

"That's for you guys to find out," Mrs. Martin said giving up "I am going to freshen up and prepare dinner."

The family dispersed from the hall and the brothers went upstairs to their room to rest until dinner was ready.

After about an hour and a half, the family sat around the dining table for dinner. Mr. Martin served the food on everyone's plates.

"You boys will be amazed to know that the Tomato soup has been prepared by me," he said as he served it to the boys and Helena.

Oswald Martin generally didn't like to cook and whenever he did so, the food often tasted bad. However, today he helped his wife as she was tired after the outing.

"Not bad, Dad," Joe admired as he put a spoon of the soup in his mouth.

"The noodles look tastier, though," John said teasing his father.

"Fine, don't have the soup then," their father replied trying to look offended.

Just then, Joe heard a rustling noise coming from the back door of the house in the kitchen.

"Heard that?" he asked John as he got up from his chair and walked silently towards the door.

John followed his younger brother without a word. Joe swiftly opened the door and looked outside.

"Hey, there's someone running away!" he exclaimed pointing at a man running towards the front of the house.

"I will seal the front," John said as he left the back door, got out of the kitchen and went into the hall towards the front door with his father following him.

Joe in the meantime stepped out of the back door and onto the backyard and gave the shady man a chase all the way to the front.

The man, however, got out of the main gate of the Martin's Residence jumped onto a scooter parked right outside and sped off. Joe reached the main gate as John and Oliver Martin emerged out of the main door and into the front yard.

"Where's he?" asked Mr. Martin.

"He just got away on a scooter," Joe said pointing towards the scooter in the horizon.

"Did you get a look at his face or the scooter?" John asked hoping to get some information about the eavesdropper.

"No," Joe replied shaking his head sideways.

"I wonder since when was he listening to our conversations," John wondered out loud.

"Probably after Mr. Bucks left," Joe said after

thinking for a moment “There was no sign of him or the scooter when he was leaving.”

“Yeah,” his father agreed “I didn’t see any scooter parked here when we arrived in the evening.”

The three concluded that the man must have come after they had all gone into the house and had most probably overheard Mr. Bucks’ story when the boys were briefing their parents about it. Presently, they updated their mother with what had happened as she herself emerged out of the front door of the house.

3

The Sweet Tooth

* * *

Joe ducked under the bed as he waited for the intruder to leave the bedroom. Generally, he would have attacked the person but this person had a gun with him. He sported a big mustache equivalent to the Punjab is in India and wore a black gown. The man who had a pretty slim figure was no less than a 6'2" height.

Joe lied down under the bed. John and his parents had gone out and Joe had overslept until he had heard the front door lock being picked. He had gone out of his room to see who it was but as soon as he saw this man with the gun, he had darted off to his room and ducked under the bed. The man had come following him into the room.

Presently, the man looked all around in the bedroom. He looked behind the curtains, checked the bathroom and even looked for Joe inside the closet. Having failed in finding him, he began walking towards the door to get out of the room. However, he suddenly stopped in his tracks seeming to remember or realize something. Then he walked over to John's bed, crouched beside it and then looked under it. There was no one. Then he got up from his position, came over to Joe's bed and crouched beside it. At this point, Joe kicked the intruder on his thighs and got out from under the bed. The man caught unaware was still trying to realize what had happened. Joe took advantage of this situation and landed a heavy blow on the man's face breaking a few teeth. He didn't stop at that. He landed a karate chop on the man's right wrist making him lose his grip on the Pistol he was holding. The Pistol fell down on the floor and Joe picked it up and pointed it at the intruder.

"Who are you?" he asked.

The tall man didn't give any reply. He landed a kick on Joe's stomach and before Joe could react, gave a sweeping blow at Joe's legs making him fall on the floor. The man picked up the Pistol and aimed it at Joe.

"Hahaha!" he laughed in a rather animated way.

"Wh…who are you?" Joe asked stammering from the pain and fear as he tried to get up onto his feet.

The man didn't reply. He locked his gun and pressed the trigger. The bullet zoomed off from the Pistol and hit Joe right at his heart. He surrendered and fell onto the floor flat waiting for death to take him. He heard a voice in the distance.

"Joe...Joe!"

John must have returned, Joe realized. He wanted to get up and warn his brother about the intruder but he had no energy to do so. He had started to feel dizzy.

"Joe…Joe...!" The voice was starting to draw closer.

John was coming towards the bedroom, Joe thought.

"Joe…! Get up, Joe!" John shook his brother as he opened his eyes.

"Oh, I was dreaming," Joe realized relieved that it was all a dream.

"I don't care," his brother said rolling his eyes "Get up now. We better get ready and have breakfast. Jeff will be here soon. We have to go to Mr. Bucks' house, remember?"

"Yes, I do," Joe said getting out of his sleep

completely and sitting on the bed “I will go freshen up.”

The Martin brothers freshened up and got ready. They then walked downstairs to the kitchen. As they entered the kitchen, they saw their mother already preparing breakfast.

“Good morning, Mom!” the two greeted.

“Good morning, dear!” Mrs. Martin wished back “You guys seem to be heading somewhere.”

“Yeah,” John replied “We are going to Mr. Bucks’ house to inspect the backyard and see if we can get any clues as to who the thieves are.”

“Well, Good luck then!” Mrs. Martin wished as she served her boys a bowl of corn flakes and a plate of toasted bread slices.

“Where is Dad?” John asked as he picked up the peanut butter to apply on his bread slices.

“He went for a bath a few minutes back,” his mother replied preparing the coffee “He will join you two soon.”

John applied peanut butter on his bread slices whereas Joe applied a mixed fruit jam.

“Did you talk to Jeff?” Joe asked John over the course of the breakfast. Their mother had joined them by now.

“No, he promised he will be here at 8 30 sharp,” John replied checking his watch. There were only a couple of minutes to 8 30.

“Good morning lads and my beautiful wife!” Mr. Martin wished as he entered the kitchen cum dining hall.

The three wished him back. Mr. Oswald Martin’s work usually started from 9 30 in the morning and went on till 6 in the evening. The previous day being a Sunday, he had the chance to take his wife on an outing but on weekdays, he rarely got the chance to do so.

“You guys going to Jean Bucks’ place?” he asked as

he joined the others with his breakfast.

The boys nodded.

"We hope to find some clues regarding the theft," John added.

"Well, all the best," his Dad wished "Be careful, though. And if you find him or them, give them a good lesson so that they never eavesdrop on people in the future," he said in a light mood referring to the incident of the previous evening.

"We sure will," Joe replied with a smirk "But we aren't sure if that man was indeed responsible for the theft at Jean Bucks' place."

Just then there was a knock on the back door in the kitchen. John who had almost finished with his breakfast got up to open the door.

"Hello, guys!" Jeff greeted with an excited and happy smile as he walked into the kitchen.

"Hi, Jeff!" the others greeted back.

"Did you have breakfast?" Helena asked.

"Yes, Aunt Helena. Some sausages and eggs."

"Come on, Mom," Joe picked on his mother "His parents love him too."

The others laughed.

In a few minutes, the brothers got ready to go.

"See you later, Mom and Dad," John and Joe bid goodbye.

"Take care," their parents replied.

They took out their bikes from the garage towards the front of the house. John owned a red Ducati Multistrada whereas Joe an orange KTM 950 Adventure. Jeff went out over to his own bike, a Cagiva Raptor 125 parked on the driveway. The three started their bikes and got out of the house's compound and onto the Sandy Street in Yorkville. They went north through the street till they reached the Ring

Road intersection and took a right turn from there onto the Ring Road. They crossed the Louisiana Fire Station, the New Heroes Memorial which was built in the remembrance of the patriots of the country and the Echo Park just after that. Once in St. Bryan's, they took a left turn onto the highway leading to Portville town and within minutes, they reached the address that Jean Bucks had written down on the notepad the previous day.

The house, which was rather a two-story mansion, looked like a run-down house from the twentieth century. It called out for an overdue of repairs with the paint coming off and cracks evidently visible on the walls. The mansion was surrounded by a concrete wall, which seemed like it could break down any moment, but however, had no gate for safety. The boys rode their bikes onto the driveway. The front yard looked to be under-maintained as well with just the area near the driveway been looked after. The further areas had weeds and long grasses growing.

"Who would think that this man has a treasure," Jeff wondered out loud seeing the state of the place.

The boys parked their motorbikes near the porch and walked up to the doorbell. Joe was just about to ring the doorbell when the main door opened.

"Hello, boys," Mr. Jean Bucks greeted with a smile "I heard the engines and figured it was you."

He was wearing a black vest revealing all his overgrown chest hair. The way he was dressed up the previous evening when he had visited the Martins' Residence, no one would have guessed that his house was such a run-down affair. The place gave an indication to the boys that the man, though had two pots of nineteenth-century treasure, was actually in a state of poverty.

Jean Bucks invited the boys in into the hall. The hall was no better than the outside. It had old paintings hanging on the walls along with some old candle stands.

The wallpapers had started to come off and the corners of the room were dusty with cobwebs here and there.

"It's difficult for a single man to look after this big house, you see," Jean Bucks specified with a sign of embarrassment on his face.

"We can understand," John said. He knew what Jean Bucks said was actually true. Such a large house was not possible to be well-maintained by a single man especially since he also had a job which made John ask.

"You didn't go to work today?"

"My shift starts at 2 in the afternoon today," Mr. Bucks replied.

Jean Bucks took the three boys to the back door which was ajar. He opened it wide revealing the big backyard.

"Wow!" Jeff admired the backyard "One could easily play football here."

Jean laughed at first and then said, "You see, land was pretty cheap in Fischerberg back then when my Great-great Grandfather bought it."

The city of Fischerberg was only established in 1899. The port came up before it in 1890 and the small town of Portville was established. However, people didn't want to live in Portville as it was a dirty and crowded town back then. So people who worked at Portville preferred to live towards the outskirts of the town which were comparatively better. The Midlands Forest which lies between Portville and Fischerberg was a source of timber back then. Woodcutters preferred to live towards the southern side of the forest rather than to live towards the north in the town of Portville. As more and more woodcutters started to reside towards the southern part of the forest, the town of Fischerberg was established. Thus, the northern parts of the city were the oldest and it spread towards the south and also towards the east and west. The timber mill was however closed in 1970 as the issue of deforestation gained importance and the industrial area was built up towards the north of Red Town and Louisiana areas to provide jobs for people and also to grow the city as an industrial hub. The city had its own airport towards the south and the river port was just 18 kilometers or a little more than 11 miles away in Portville. Hence, it had all the requisites to become a major industrial hub.

Presently, Jean Bucks took the boys into the backyard of his mansion. The boys were awe stricken by the huge size of the backyard. It measured almost the full width of a soccer field from the house to fence at the rear.

"Haven't you received any offer to sell this house?" Jeff asked out of curiosity. The place could easily be used for some commercial offices or small plazas.

"I received a couple of offers last year, but I rejected them," Mr. Bucks replied.

"Why?" Jeff continued "Did they not offer you a good price?"

"It's not always about money, my child," Mr. Bucks replied in his usual husky voice "This mansion is a family heirloom. Anyway, I have no children. So once I die, I don't know what will happen to this place. However, till the time I am alive, I will look after this place."

The boys felt sorry for Mr. Bucks' situation. Living all alone in this huge mansion with no one to talk to must be so lonely in itself. And above that, he didn't seem to have many friends or relatives.

"Come, I will take you to the spot where the treasure was stolen from," Jean Bucks offered "I haven't covered the pit yet thinking you would want to have a look at it."

He led the way towards the north of the compound. The backyard was full of long grass and weeds. Only a part of it seemed to be some sort of a kitchen garden which was again very under-maintained. They soon arrived at a pit of about 3 feet deep. The soil dug out from it lay on the sides of it.

"This is where the pot was," Mr. Bucks said pointing at the hole.

Something in the hole caught John's eyes. He bent down and picked up a small piece of wrapper.

"Seems like a toffee wrapper," John said examining it.

He straightened it and read the name on it.

"Sweet-o," he read out from the wrapper.

"Do you have these toffees, Mr. Bucks?" Jeff asked trying to figure out if he had dropped it mistakenly.

"No, I don't have toffees at all," Mr. Bucks replied.

"Do you have any gardener or anyone else who comes to the backyard?" Joe asked.

"Not at all," the fifty-year-old replied "I don't let anyone come to the backyard apart from my friends. But I can assure you that none of my friends visited me in the past few days."

"Then this wrapper sure belongs to the thieves," concluded John.

"So that's our first clue then," Joe said happily at the fact that they had got something out of this trip to Mr. Bucks' place.

The boys looked around for some more time hoping to find more clues or more of the same chocolate wrappers but it yielded no result. Finally, after about an hour of search, the boys decided to leave. They exchanged goodbyes with Jean Bucks and hopped onto their bikes parked outside.

"Do let me know if you find something," Mr. Bucks called out as the boys rode off.

The three Js followed the same route they had taken earlier to reach the Martins' residence.

"I will go home, have lunch and then come over to your place to discuss the case," Jeff said as they reached John and Joe's place.

"Sure," John agreed "We sure need to discuss the case."

Jeff rode off towards his home and the brothers parked their bikes at the garage. The car wasn't there. The boys figured their Dad must have taken it to work. Mr. Martin generally went to work in the office cab but once in a while, he loved to take his own car to work. Presently, John and Joe went towards the back of the house and entered through the open back door in the kitchen.

"Hi, Mom!" they greeted as they entered the kitchen.

"Hi, boys!" Mrs. Martin greeted back amid the preparation of lunch "How was the investigation?"

"It was pretty good," John replied, "We probably found our first clue."

"Oh and what's that?" his mother asked.

"We will brief you later. First tell us, what's there for lunch today?" Joe asked starting to feel a little hungry.

"Salad, steak and fries," Mrs. Helena Martin replied still frying the fries "They will be ready in ten minutes. Go upstairs and freshen up."

The boys did as told. After twenty minutes they met their mother downstairs in the kitchen who was serving lunch for the three.

"Oh, I found a chocolate wrapper near the back door today morning," the boys' mother said as soon as she saw them enter the kitchen "I kept it for you boys to check. You guys certainly wouldn't throw a wrapper there so I felt maybe it belonged to yesterday's eavesdropper."

She produced a wrapper similar to the one the boys found in the pit at Mr. Bucks' backyard. John took it and examined it.

"Sweet-o," he said reading the name on the wrapper.

"So it was probably one of the thieves who was eavesdropping at our home yesterday," Joe inferred.

The boys told their mother about the similar type of toffee wrapper they had found in the pit where the treasure pot was at Mr. Bucks' backyard.

"So the thieves know that Mr. Bucks came here to talk to you guys about the theft," Mrs. Martin guessed once the boys had concluded.

"Possibly," John replied, "Moreover, he also knows that there is another pot in that backyard because he must have overheard us telling you and Dad about it."

"So he probably will attempt another theft," Joe determined.

"Right," John agreed.

"I think you guys should warn Mr. Bucks that you feel the thieves would visit him again," Mrs. Martin suggested.

The boys agreed and John went over to the hall to call their client.

"I also received a mail today in your name," Mrs. Martin said suddenly remembering "It's there beside the telephone."

Joe went to the hall, walked up to the telephone where John was already making the call and picked up the envelope from beside it. He checked it to see who the sender was but there was no sender's address. He tore open the envelope and produced a small white strip of paper from inside it.

As he read the paper, his eyes were filled with shock and suspicion. John, who had by now told Mr. Jean Bucks everything, presently said goodbye to him and kept the receiver down. He at first didn't notice Joe' change in expression but soon enough, realized Joe's face wasn't the natural.

"What happened, Joe?" he asked eager to know the reason behind Joe's reaction.

Joe handed over the paper to John for him to read it. It said,

'Get off the case right now. We know where you live and would leave no chance in harming your family if you don't let us do our job.'

4

A Little Hope...

* * *

"Now they look a little dangerous," John said.

The boys had initially thought that the people they were dealing with were just some petty thieves who somehow found out about the treasure and stole it but the threatening note and especially that they mentioned they would harm their family put some fear into the boys. It wasn't that the boys hadn't got threats like these in their previous cases, but just as a Goalkeeper always felt nervous about facing a penalty shootout, no matter how many times he had faced one in the past, the boys felt a little scared in spite of receiving numerous threats like these in the past.

"We will have to be careful," Joe decided.

"Right," John agreed "Let's warn Mom about it."

The boys went into the kitchen where their mother was placing the plates on the dining table.

"Lunch is ready," she said as the boys entered the kitchen "Come sit."

The boys took their seats and explained her in turns about the note and why they thought that she and their father needed to be careful, especially when they were not at home.

"Ok, now it looks like there's danger involved," Mrs. Martin said once they boys had completed explaining.

"Yes," Joe replied "So we suggest you and Dad to be careful. Keep the doors closed whenever possible."

"That's not a problem," their mother said reassuringly and then added with a concerned voice "But I am worried about you two. They can harm you guys as well."

"We will be fine, Mom," John assured her as Joe nodded in agreement "We can take care of ourselves."

"I know you can but you don't know how many of them are there," Mrs. Martin said with a worried face "You certainly can't take care of yourselves if there are ten men against you."

The boys knew that what their mother had said was absolutely true and in fact, they themselves were worried. But to reassure their mother, they insisted that they would be fine and safe.

"Ok, just take care of yourselves," Mrs. Martin said still worried.

The three finished their lunch soon and the boys helped their Mom with the dishes and to clean the table. Later, John and Joe went upstairs to their room after making sure for once that both the front door and the back door were properly locked.

"Jeff should be here soon," Joe said checking the time. It was almost 2 pm.

"I wonder why the thieves were eavesdropping yesterday," John wondered out loud.

"They must have found out somehow that Mr. Bucks visited us and that we were asked to help him."

"Do you think they were following Mr. Bucks when he came here?"

"Could be. You cannot rule that out."

Just then the door bell rang. John got up and went downstairs to see who it was. Mrs. Martin was already there and was opening the door by then.

"Hi, Jeff," Helena Martin greeted as she invited the young lad in and closed the door behind him.

"Hi, Aunt Helena," Jeff greeted back "I came over to discuss the case with John and Joe."

"OK," Mrs. Martin said, "Just be careful. John will tell you why."

As John accompanied his cousin upstairs he told him everything about the toffee wrapper his mother had found in the morning and also about the threatening mail they had received.

"Wow!" exclaimed Jeff as the two entered the Martin brothers' room "It's heating up from here."

"It certainly is," John agreed.

"Hey, Jeff," Joe greeted his cousin brother.

"Hello, Joe," Jeff greeted back, "John told me about the mail. We need to be careful from now."

"Yes, that's correct. Why don't you call up your home and warn them as well?" John suggested, "The thieves might go there as well."

"I never thought of that," Jeff said realizing that what John said could actually be correct "I will call up Mom right away."

He took out his cell phone from his pocket and dialed the number to his home and told his mother everything about the threatening note.

"Who do you think could have stolen the treasure?" Joe asked once Jeff was done warning his mother.

"I have no idea. We have no suspects so far," Jeff replied.

"Let's do some research on the Romanian-Russian protocol," John suggested, "We might find something useful in case there is a historic angle involved in this."

Joe and Jeff looked over John's shoulder as he switched on the computer and searched for the Romanian transfer of national treasure. They kept surfing and reading articles for a few minutes.

"Hey, look," Jeff said pointing to a line in one of the articles "During World War II, the Soviet Government transferred all the treasure out of Moscow to some other area which was thought to be less endangered."

"I wonder where but obviously in Russia itself," Joe suggested.

"Some chests of archives were sent back to Romania in 1935 but they looked like they had been rummaged through and many documents and objects were missing," John read out from another article.

"Do you think the Soviets stole some of the Romanian treasure?" Jeff asked suspiciously.

"It sure looks that way. In fact not 'some', they kept 'most' of it to themselves," Joe replied.

"Another line here says that post the fall of USSR, the Russian Government's stance on the issue remained the same and only some of the cultural heritage and artifacts were returned but none of the Jewelry or Gold treasure amid various failed negotiations," John read out.

"That means the more valuable items were never returned," Joe quipped.

"True," John agreed "It's sad the Romanians didn't see it coming when they made the decision to send their treasure out."

"They had no other option, remember what Mr. Bucks had said?" Jeff remembered, "They couldn't send it to other countries because the Germans would seize it and to keep it in their own country in itself was very risky."

"Well, this gives us an insight into the history but nothing much for the case we are working on," Joe pointed out.

"Right," John agreed and turned on his chair to face the other two.

"What I don't understand is how did the thieves know the pinpoint location of the treasure?" Jeff wondered out loud "I mean, Mr. Bucks told us that he didn't let anyone go to the backyard neither did he tell anyone about the treasure as it was a well-kept family secret."

"That's something that has been puzzling me as well," John admitted.

"He must have told someone about it," Joe suggested, "Maybe some close friend or relative."

"Could be," Jeff agreed "Another thing is when they were digging the treasure out that night, didn't Mr. Bucks hear anything? That place is usually exceptionally silent at night."

"Jeff's got a point," Joe admitted, "Do you think Mr. Bucks himself is as clean as we think him to be?"

"Let's not assume he isn't clean at the moment," John suggested "We will ask him the next time we meet him. There ought to be some explanation."

"Possibly," Jeff agreed "Besides I don't see any motive for Mr. Bucks to make up this false case."

"Come to think of a motive, what would be your motive behind stealing an ancient treasure if you were a thief?" John asked thinking.

"Sell the treasure and get money, obviously," Joe replied.

"Seems legit," John said, "So the thieves must have sold all or some of the treasure to someone in return for money."

"A jewelry store?" Jeff suggested.

"Yes," agreed Joe "But won't they get suspicious on seeing the ancient gold bars or jewelry?"

"Most won't," John quipped "People often sell their ancient family gold and jewelry in return for money. If the thieves took the full pot to one single store, the merchant would become suspicious, but if they took just a little bit of it to sell, they would face no problem."

"Let's look for all the Jewelry stores and shortlist them on the basis of which one offers the most money," Joe suggested.

"Agreed," Jeff said agreeing to the idea "We will get to know about which shops offer the most money from the customer reviews."

John turned back towards the computer and started looking for all the major Jewelry stores in Fischerberg. The boys read the reviews of each store that they could find and finally after about a couple of hours of work zeroed in on ten shops.

"There, the list is done then," Joe declared as he penned down the last shop.

"So how about we go to each of these shops and ask the people there about the gold and the jewelry?" Jeff suggested.

"Cool," John and Joe agreed.

The brothers bid goodbye to their mother and were soon riding off on their respective bikes to the shops. The three divided the shops among themselves based on the areas where the shops were. John took the areas of Dillinore and South Central towards the south of Fishcerberg whereas Joe took the areas of Central Fischerberg and Stone Lake for himself. Jeff was given responsibility for the areas of Drake, North Luis Santos, and Downtown towards the south-eastern parts of Fischerberg. Each of them got three shops to check except Jeff who had an extra shop. They decided to call each other via their cell phones if any one of them found out anything.

The three Js went from shop to shop but found no positive results. Soon Jeff walked into the third store on his list. The shop named 24 Carat, on the Heather way Street in North Luis Santos looked a rather old and comparatively small shop having just one customer at present. Jeff walked up to the store manager who seemed to be in his late thirties. The man had a bulgy stomach and was munching on some fries, mayonnaise, and coffee. His hair had started to fall off and there was hair only at the back of his head.

"Hello, I am Jeff Martin," Jeff greeted.

"Hello, sir," the store manager replied amid a sip of his coffee "Dillon Johnson. How may I help you?"

"I came to ask you about a thief," Jeff started "He recently stole some gold and jewelry from a house and I suspect he might have come here to sell them. You see there's a bounty on his head as well. The stuff that he stole was mostly old Romanian riches from the nineteenth century."

He falsely mentioned about the bounty to spur some interest from the store manager.

"But who are you?" Mr. Johnson asked doubtfully.

"I am a private detective," Jeff replied "I work along with John and Joe Martin and are called the three Js commonly. We are currently working on a case for a client."

"I see," the manager said appearing to think of something "Yes, I do remember reading somewhere about the three Js. Now that you've mentioned about Romanian gold, yes, two men came today in the morning soon after I opened the store with a few gold ornaments and jewelry. When I asked where they got them, they replied that these belonged to their family. I gave them quite a good price as the stuff seemed authentic. I didn't know it was stolen loot."

"It's ok," Jeff assured him "Can you give me back the stuff?"

"No, I paid a huge amount of money for that," the manager retorted, "You can pay me that sum and take it back."

"How much?"

"Seventeen thousand five hundred dollars."

Jeff paused for a moment. That was a huge amount of money and he wasn't sure if Mr. Bucks could afford to pay that much money.

"Ok," Jeff said finally "You'll get the money in a few days. Just don't sell them to anyone."

"Done," replied Mr. Johnson seeming satisfied.

"Tell me more about the thieves," Jeff asked coming back to the main motive for his visit "Do you remember anything about them? How they looked like or anything at all."

"Umm…no," the manager responded after trying to remember for some time "But one of them was wearing a baseball cap."

"Anything else?" Jeff asked. The information he had acquired so far wasn't enough for them to track the thieves.

"Oh yes," Dillon Johnson said remembering something suddenly "They were very happy with the price I offered. So they said that they would be back tomorrow with a few more of the gold and jewels. They said they wanted money for their mother's treatment."

"Great!" Jeff exclaimed happily with the news that they would come back the next day "So they are coming tomorrow?"

"Right," the manager replied "Come in the morning. They will probably come here in the morning just as they did today. You see I don't get many customers in the morning or in the afternoon, so I guess, they chose that time."

"Sure, Mr. Johnson," Jeff agreed "When do you open store?"

"I open the store at around 9 30. They came at around 10 in the morning. I suggest you come at 9 30 itself. Then you can nab them when they arrive."

"That's awesome, Mr. Johnson," Jeff said still excited about the fact that they may actually nab the thieves the next day "Thank you so much for your help. I will see you tomorrow then."

Jeff walked out of the store and called John.

"Hey, Jeff!" John greeted as he received the call "What's up? Found anything?"

"Yes, I did," Jeff replied still excited.

"What is it?" John asked full of expectation.

"I will tell you soon," Jeff replied "Meet me at my place as soon as possible. Tell Joe as well."

"Ok," John replied "Seems cool. See you then."

5

...And Lots of Danger

* * *

Jeff got onto his bike and roared off towards his home in Yorkville. He reached there in about 40 minutes. As he parked his motorcycle in the garage of the Martin's Abode, he noticed John and Joe's bikes in the driveway. He expected them to reach before him anyway because the areas which were under John and Joe's responsibility were much closer to Yorkville than North Luis Santos where Jeff had found the valuable piece of information.

Presently, he walked up to the porch of the house and rang the bell. The house was a typical American Bungalow with slanted roofs at the top. It had a small porch in the front and a hall, a dining hall cum kitchen and two bedrooms inside it. There was a comparatively smaller room upstairs which was used as a small study by Mr. Walter Martin, Jeff's father and Oswald Martin's brother, who worked at the district library in North Austrot towards the southwest of Fischerberg City. The front yard of the house was decorated with a smooth lawn surrounded by beautiful seasonal flowers including Periwinkle and Daisies.

"Hey, Jeff," Joe greeted as he opened the door.

Jeff greeted him back and walked into the hall. The hall was medium sized with a fireplace towards one side. The walls had recently been applied new wallpapers which gave it a relatively new look. The hall consisted of a brown English sofa set accompanied by a center table. Mrs. Claudia Martin Jeff's mother, who had a hobby of gardening and loved flowers, had decorated the hall with beautiful indoor plants.

However, at present, Mrs. Claudia Martina long with the boys carried a worried expression on their face.

"What happened, Mom?" Jeff asked sensing that something was wrong.

"I am glad you are fine, son," Mrs. Martin revealed somewhat relieved.

"Why?" Jeff asked surprised "What would happen to me?"

John produced a note and a round and smooth rock which was the size of an average fist. He handed the note to Jeff. Jeff read the note which said –

'We guessed you boys would not stop with one warning. So here is another one to let you know that we are indeed serious. Back off from the case or else you know what will happen.'

"Another threat!" Jeff exclaimed once he had finished reading.

"Someone threw this note wrapped on the rock John is holding through the window in the hall," Mrs. Martin said with a worried face and then pointing at one of the windows said, "Look, the pane is broken."

"Are these men following us?" Jeff wondered out loud.

"We will get the answer to that only once we catch them, I guess," John replied.

"The rock they threw in is pretty big to hurt someone," Joe admitted, "It could have easily hurt anyone who would be struck by it."

"You are right," Jeff realized "These men sure seem serious."

"I just want you guys to be careful," Claudia Martin said still worried "the window can be fixed, that's no problem. In fact, I have already called the repairman. But you boys should be careful. Whoever these men are, they sure look dangerous."

"At least they don't own a weapon, I hope," Joe guessed.

"You never know," John replied, "But I really hope they don't."

The fact that the men could own weapons as well seemed to worry Jeff's mother even more.

"Do you think it's too dangerous for your own good?" she asked.

"No, Aunt Claudia," John replied in a convincing voice "We will be fine."

"We sure will," Jeff added, "These men don't know how good detectives we can be."

"Anyway, I will go to the kitchen to prepare dinner," Mrs. Martin said finally "Do you want to have dinner here, John and Joe?"

"No, thank you, Aunt Claudia," the brothers replied in unison.

The three then went to Jeff's room so that he could tell the Martin brothers why he had called them here. Once they were comfortably seated on Jeff's bed and the computer chair, Jeff briefed them about what he had learned at the store named 24 Carat. He told them about Mr. Dillon Johnson, about the money he had paid for the loot and also that he was expecting the thieves to be there the next day.

"Wow!" Joe exclaimed once the young lad had finished briefing "That's quite a find, Jeff."

"I know," Jeff admitted, "The only problem is can

Mr. Bucks arrange for seventeen thousand and five hundred dollars?"

"You are right," John agreed "He didn't seem to be one who would have that much money in his bank account. His only wealth it seems is the old Romanian treasure, which he isn't going to spend."

"I will call him up and tell him about it nonetheless once we go home," Joe offered.

"Ok," John agreed "So we have a good chance to catch the thieves tomorrow!"

"Right," Jeff said excitedly "We will leave at around 8:30 from here. Mr. Johnson opens his shop at 9:30 in the morning."

"Oh, I almost forgot," John said suddenly remembering something "I have to go meet Mr. Vance Ice, my professor at the academy regarding the project I am currently working on. So I won't be able to join you guys tomorrow."

"It's ok," Jeff assured, "Joe and I will nab those men."

"Roger that," Joe agreed.

The boys talked on for a few more minutes before deciding to call it a night. John and Joe exchanged good nights with their cousin and his mother and left for their home which was just round the corner.

By the time the boys reached their home, it was almost dinner time. Joe called up Mr. Bucks to tell him about what they had learned from the store manager.

"That's a pretty hefty amount," their client said when he heard the price of his treasure.

"I know," Joe admitted, "But he is demanding that much for returning the gold and jewels."

"I will see what I can do and try to arrange for the money," Mr. Bucks said "Good luck to you in catching the thieves tomorrow."

"Thank you, Mr. Bucks," Joe thanked as he kept the

receiver down.

Then the boys freshened up and sat for dinner with their parents. There were soup and fried rice for dinner. Over the course of the dinner, the boys briefed their parents about what Jeff had found out.

"That's good news," Mr. Martin said with a smile "Good luck for tomorrow. Just be careful."

"Thanks, Dad," the brothers replied in unison.

At Jeff's house, they were having a dinner of ordered pizza.

"These men seem pretty dangerous," Mr. Walter Martin admitted, "We need to be careful."

"Yes, Dad," Jeff agreed "You are right. Anyway, we will hopefully catch them tomorrow."

"Claudia," Mr. Martin said turning to his wife "You stay alone at home in the day especially because Jeff goes out with John and Joe to investigate. You should be extra careful."

"I will," his wife nodded in agreement "I was pretty scared when I heard the rock crashing in through the window today. I was even scared to go out and check who it was. But after a few minutes, John and Joe arrived, and I felt much more comfortable."

"I think I should tell the cops about it," Walter Martin figured.

"No, Dad," Jeff said stopping his Dad "Don't do that. The information about the treasure is supposed to remain a secret. If we tell the cops about the rock, they will learn everything about Mr. Bucks' treasure."

That seemed to stop the man from calling the police but he said that they should all be very cautious.

Next morning, Joe woke up after 7 and had a shower. Then he got ready and went downstairs for breakfast along with John. John was supposed to go to the academy at around 9 to meet his Professor and so he too had freshened up.

"Be sure to catch them today, Joe," John said as he munched on his waffles.

"We sure will," Joe assured, "Don't worry."

"Be careful, though," Mr. Martin suggested, "They may have weapons and be dangerous."

"We will be careful, Dad," Joe assured his father.

Soon breakfast was over and Joe said goodbye to his parents and John who wished him good luck in return. He walked over to the garage at the front to take out his bike and to go to Jeff's house. John would leave for the academy later. Just as Joe was taking out his bike, a 125 cc bike stopped right in front of the Martins' residence.

"Ready, Joe?" Jeff asked from over his bike.

"Yeah," Joe replied as he got onto his bike and started it "Let's go."

The boys went south through the Sandy Street for some time and then took a left turn onto the Adam's Avenue. They then went east on it as they crossed Dillinore, and South Central on their way. Soon they reached Urn Town, where they took a left turn and headed north till the Irin's Circle, named after the Irin's park situated nearby. The brothers took the first exit onto the Heather way street and headed east via it. After another 5 minutes, they reached North Luis Santos and about another five minutes later, they reached the shop of their interest, the one named 24 Carat. The whole journey had taken them almost an hour and by the time they reached, the shop had already opened.

Presently, the boys parked their bikes outside and went into the shop. The shop had no customers at the moment and Mr. Dillon Johnson was reading the newspaper with a cup of hot chocolate beside him on the counter.

"Good morning, Mr. Johnson," Jeff greeted as they went up to the manager.

"Oh, hello," Mr. Johnson greeted back.

"This is Joe Martin, my cousin brother," Jeff introduced him to Mr. Johnson.

"Hello, lad," Mr. Johnson replied, "I have sure read about you two."

"Did the men visit you today?" Joe asked getting to the point.

"No no," the manager replied, "But they should be here soon."

The boys decided to look around the store at the different pieces of jewelry to pass time. They were amazed by the vast types of ornaments and their price which were stated to be from as low as a few dollars to as high as some thousands of dollars. As they were exploring around, Joe got the urge to answer nature's call. He walked up to the store manager.

"Uh, Mr. Johnson, where can I find the washroom?" he asked.

"It's at the back room of the store," Mr. Johnson replied pointing at a door towards the rear side of the store which said 'Only Authorized Personnel' "Take a right from there, you will see the signboard of the washroom."

"Thank you," Joe thanked and went up to the door Mr. Johnson had pointed at.

He opened the door and walked into a dimly lit room which took Joe's eyes a few moments to adjust from the morning sunlight and bright lights at the store. At the first look, the room seemed like a shady hideout from some movie which was used as an office room for some undercover secret agency. It had a table and a chair and a few file cabinets around along with some photos and a sales chart hanging on the wall.

'This must be Mr. Johnson's office,' Joe thought.

He soon saw the signboard to the washroom placed above a door towards his right. As he walked towards it, something else caught his eyes. Joe noticed a loose tile under the desk. The loose tile was somewhat different from the other ones in the room and was bulging out from the rest. Realizing that there was no one else in the room, Joe's curiosity got the better of him and he went up to the desk and crouched beside it. He examined the tile for a few moments and then checked if it would come out. It did. There was a pit of around 4 feet under the tile and it spread sideways as well. Joe took out his cell phone and used it's flashlight to examine the pit. It had a few bags containing some gold and jewelry.

'So this is Mr. Johnson's secret locker,' Joe thought amused by the store manager's creativity.

He checked a few bags to see if he could find Mr. Bucks' treasure that the men had sold to this store, but he was unable to recognize them. He soon placed the loose tile back in its original position. He made sure that the tile was bulging out of the other tiles just like it was initially. Once he had achieved that, he went to the washroom.

"Did the men arrive yet?" Joe asked Jeff as he walked out of the back room.

"Not yet," Jeff replied shaking his head sideways.

"I hope they are actually coming today," Joe said.

"They should," Jeff replied, "That's what Mr. Johnson said."

Just then, the door of the store opened and a man who seemed to be in his late twenties or early thirties walked in. He had a wedge hair and was sporting a sunglass. The man, rather slim and approximately the height of Joe and Jeff had a small bag in his hands.

But then suddenly, he stopped in his tracks and seeing the two boys in the store he darted out.

"That was one of them, boys," Mr. Johnson said eagerly pointing towards the front door.

Joe and Jeff didn't need another invitation. They zoomed out of the shop and gave the running man a chase.

The man took them around the block and then crossed the road to another block. The two Js in hot pursuit had started to gain in on the fugitive. Presently, the man again turned around the block and then went into an alleyway. The boys followed but by the time they reached the alleyway, the man was nowhere to be seen.

"Where did he go?" Jeff wondered out loud.

"He must be hiding somewhere here," Joe replied, "We will find him."

But before the boys could start their search, Joe heard a loud sound beside him of something hitting someone and saw Jeff's body fall onto the ground. Before Joe could react, though, he heard a similar sound as he felt a blow on the back of his head by something hard and dizziness crossed over him as he too fell down on the ground and lost consciousness.

6

A Gaseous Affair

* * *

A pungent smell woke Joe up. Wincing in pain he tried to feel the back of his head but he realized he couldn't move his hand. He opened his eyes but all that he could see was black. It took a moment for him to realize that his hands and legs were tied up. However, his mouth wasn't gagged.

"Jeff?" he called out in a low whisper.

There was no answer. The faint pungent smell in the air grabbed his attention. Joe tried to figure out what the smell was but his mind didn't seem to work. All he could feel was the throbbing pain in the back of his head where he had been hit. He guessed he might have been hit with a rod, possibly wooden because had it been of steel or iron, he wouldn't have survived. This derivation made Joe assume that whoever had hit, tied and trapped them here, had no intention to kill them. This assumption made Joe feel a bit relaxed that at least his life was safe.

All this thinking awoke Joe's mind a little and it didn't take him long to guess what the smell was. A look of horror struck his face as he finally realized what the smell was.

"Jeff?" he called again. This time his voice was stronger and he managed to push out a loud whisper.

Joe heard some rustling sound across him as something moved. He couldn't see a single thing and he was not even sure if there was darkness all around or if he had turned blind.

"Jeff?" he called again his voice getting stronger every time "Can you hear me?"

"Uh..." he heard a faint quivering voice from across him "Wh...where am I?"

"I don't know," Joe replied, "Are you alright?"

"Not at all," Jeff replied with the same faint voice "I can't seem to move my hands or legs. I can't see a thing and there is a really bad pain in the back of my head."

"We were hit, tied and brought here," Joe explained, "And now we are trapped at this place."

The fact that Jeff too couldn't see made Joe sure that at least he hadn't turned blind. There was indeed darkness all around.

"I can see that we are trapped somewhere," Jeff said, his voice getting a little stronger now "But where?"

"How am I supposed to know?" Joe said feeling uneasy "I too was knocked out."

"Oh ok," Jeff said. Then as he got the same pungent smell, he demanded, "What is that smell?"

"It seems to be coming from a leaking LPG gas," Joe replied feeling a lot more uneasy now.

"Oh no!" Jeff said with a horrified voice. His voice had become normal by now "We need to escape somehow."

"I know," Jeff agreed "But only if we can untie these ropes first."

"Maybe we can untie each other?" Jeff suggested "Our legs or hands aren't tied to anything. So we can still move with a little effort."

"That could work," Joe agreed as he tried to crawl towards where Jeff's voice was coming from.

The idea seemed difficult at first with Joe having to put too much effort to bend his legs and then straighten it to move ahead like a worm. However, as he kept trying, it became a bit easier as all his bending and straightening probably loosened the ropes around his legs.

Presently, Joe reached Jeff's body.

"Turn around so that our backs are towards each other," Joe said.

With some effort, Jeff finally turned around and both boys sat with their backs facing each other.

"I will try to untie your hands first," Joe offered.

He meddled with the ropes on Jeff's hands for some time trying to find a loose end. He pulled at the ropes trying to loosen them. This went on for quite some time without much success.

"Hurry up, Joe," Jeff said with a worried voice "The smell's getting stronger. The room is filling up with the gas."

The brothers knew that if they didn't hurry and couldn't escape in time, they both would be burnt alive by the explosion that would take place once the room was completely filled with the gas.

"Let's exchange roles," Joe suggested, "The ropes around my hands might be a bit looser than the ones around your hands."

Jeff now tried to open the ropes around Joe's hands. He ran his fingers on the ropes hoping to find a comparatively loose part. He soon succeeded in finding what he was looking for and pulled on the ropes in that location. He repeated pulled at the ropes for a few minutes until the ropes loosened significantly for Joe to free himself.

Joe stretched the ropes with his hands and was soon free. He then untied his legs and then turned to Jeff to untie his hands. Once Jeff's hands were free, he untied his legs himself.

The smell of the gas had started to become stronger as the gas started to fill the closed room.

"Now we need a way to escape," Jeff said once he was completely free.

"There ought to be some way," Joe said thinking hard as to what could be done.

"I will try finding the cylinder," Jeff suggested, "If we turn off its knob, then we will gain ourselves more time to think of an escape."

"Right," Joe agreed. He then felt for his jeans pocket saying, "I will help you. But first, let me call John and update him."

"Don't use your phone now," Jeff quipped "You really shouldn't with this gas around. In fact, let's switch them off."

"We are safe in that regard," Joe said sighing "They stole our phones."

"Right," Jeff replied feeling miserable as he felt his jeans pocket "Let's look for the cylinder."

The boys started to feel their way around in the darkness. They often bumped at the wall or at each other. They came across a table, a chair and some empty boxes which felt like they were old and used. Soon, Joe felt something curved and metallic with a hissing sound coming from it.

"Here's the cylinder," Joe called out from the other side of the room from where Jeff was. He rushed towards Joe cautiously so as to not trip over something and get himself hurt which could make matters worse.

"Great!" Jeff said with a sense of victory in his face "Find the knob and turn it off."

Joe felt for the knob of the cylinder to turn it off.

"It's no use," Joe said surrendering after a few

moments "The knob is broken. It won't turn off."

"What?" Jeff exclaimed with shock "They must have purposefully done that."

Joe felt heart-broken as his assumption that the men didn't want them dead was proved wrong. The men did indeed want to kill them. A sense of fear sank down into the boys. They were completely trapped with the leaking gas and had become really depressed. How convenient it was for the thieves to trap him and Jeff there and let them go up in flames. The whole incident would seem like an accident and no one would ever have any direct evidence against the men for murder.

"We will have to look for a way to escape," Jeff said impatiently as the smell became stronger and stronger every passing moment. He didn't want to lose hope just as yet.

"Follow the walls and look for a door or window," Joe said with a sense of impatience in his voice as he tried to find the wall himself.

The boys followed the walls feeling them with their hands for any doors or window. The room where they were, however, didn't seem to have any windows at all. This made Joe and Jeff assume that they were probably in a godown, garage or maybe even a shed.

"This seems to be a door," Jeff called out after some time.

"Can you feel what it is made of?" Joe asked rushing towards Jeff. The smell of the gas had grown very strong by now and it looked like the place would go up in blaze any moment.

"It seems like wood," Jeff replied feeling it with his fingers.

"There's hope for us then," Joe said, "Look for any loose planks."

The two felt the door vigorously for any loose plank of wood. The door had a width of almost 1.5 meters and a height of around 2.5 meters. The boys examined each and every part of the door.

"This plank seems a bit old and loose," Joe exclaimed excited at his find "I will try to break it."

"I stumbled on a chair some time back," Jeff said, "Let's try to break the plank with that."

"Ok, hurry," Joe agreed.

As Jeff went to get the chair, Joe kept trying to pull and push the plank with his hands trying to break it. He even slammed on it with his fist and kicked it with his legs but it yielded little result.

"Here it is," Jeff said starting to feel a little suffocated. The place had no openings and so the problem of oxygen shortage was looming over them as well.

Joe took the chair from Jeff, felt the plank with his hand to approximate where he had to hit and then with all his force hit the chair on the door. It produced a cracking sound as a beam of light flickered in from a tiny crack near the plank.

"Voila!" Jeff exclaimed thrilled "Let me give it a shot."

He took the chair from Joe and repeated what Joe had done. The crack became bigger as the plank loosened. However with every blow, the chair, which was itself made of wood, too had weakened and its parts were starting to become loose.

"Leave the chair," Joe said after a few more blows from Jeff "We will try to get that plank out with our hands."

As Jeff placed the chair at the side, Joe tried pulling off the plank with all his might. His finger hurt with cuts all over his palms. That didn't stop the young boy, however. He kept on pulling at the plank and finally within moments, the plank gave way and Joe flung backward and fell down on the floor with the thrust he was pulling.

Fresh air rushed in and the gas started to go out

into the open.

"Great work, Joe," Jeff congratulated his cousin brother with a pat on his back after he had helped Joe get up onto his feet.

"That opening is not big enough for us to escape,though," Joe pointed out.

"Doesn't matter," Jeff said, "at least it gives us fresh oxygen and most importantly, the gas can escape."

The two boys relaxed for some time reflecting on their achievement, to get their energy back.

"I will pull off another plank right next to the opening," Jeff offered after a few moments "That much space will be enough for us to get out of here."

"Go ahead," Joe said still feeling exhausted.

Jeff pulled and pulled on the plank towards the left of the opening Joe had managed to make. He punched at it and hit it with his shoulder until finally, the plank loosened. Then he put all his might in pulling the plank and within moments, he had managed to pull the second plank out as well.

"That's good enough, Jeff," Joe said feeling a bit refreshed.

"Let's get out of here," Jeff said, "My head and hands hurt."

"Same here," Joe sighed.

The brothers realized they were in a small shed behind an old abandoned house once they got out.

"Do you think this house is the thieves' hideout?" Jeff asked.

"I don't think so," Joe replied "They wouldn't have let the shed catch fire otherwise. The fire would have spread and gobbled up their hideout too."

"You're right," Jeff agreed "Let's get home."

"They stole my wallet as well," Joe said feeling his back pocket.

"Mine too," Jeff said realizing his wallet was missing as well "We can't take a taxi then."

The boys got out of the compound of the house and realized they were on a deserted street in North-west Fischerberg. Yorkville was just towards the east and their houses were well within walking distance. Jeff looked at the setting sun and led Joe towards the east. The boys though tired, exhausted and bruised, kept on walking motivated from the fact that they were safe and sound. They had managed to escape certain death due to their presence of mind and bravery.

After about fifteen minutes of walking, the boys reached their respective homes. Joe walked up to the door and rang the doorbell.

"What happened to you, Joe?" Mrs. Helena Martin asked with shock as soon as she saw Joe bruised and exhausted.

"It's a long story, Mom," Joe replied as he stepped into the house "I will go freshen up first."

Joe went upstairs to the bathroom and took a shower. He then applied some ointment on the bruises on his palms. Then he got into fresh clothes and walked downstairs to the hall where his brother and mother were already waiting.

"Come, sit here, dear," Mrs. Martin said affectionately.

Joe went and sat on the couch beside his mother. John was seated on the single sofa across them.

"You didn't catch them, did you?" John asked quite confidently from Joe's state.

"Nope," Joe replied as he shook his head sideways "I will tell you everything from the start."

Joe briefed Mrs. Martin and John about everything from the chase of the thief to being hit on the head and then getting trapped in the shed. He also told them about the leaky gas and how they had managed to get out of there.

"Oh God!" Mrs. Martin said horrified once Joe had finished "I am so glad you are fine."

"Those men are really dangerous," John said worried "I didn't think they would try to take someone's life. I just thought they were some petty thieves but after what happened with you and Jeff today, I really think otherwise."

"I am just glad you're fine," Mrs. Martin said still horrified "How is Jeff? Is he ok?"

"He is ok, Mom," Joe replied "Just some bruises is all that we got. Otherwise, we are fine."

"Thank your stars," John pointed out "Had it not been for you and Jeff's presence of mind…"

He refrained from finishing the sentence.

"I know," Joe said "But we are fine. So let's look ahead."

"No," his mother said in quite a firm voice "These men seem pretty dangerous for my liking. I think you should call up Mr. Bucks and tell him that you are backing off."

"No, Mom," Joe argued "We are fine. Besides we were so close to nabbing one of them. Next time, we aren't going to miss."

"Joe's right," John added "We have faced dangers while solving other cases as well."

"None of them which tried to kill you," Mrs. Martin pointed out.

The boys knew she was speaking the fact but they had to somehow convince her that they would be fine. It would be an end to this case otherwise.

"I'll tell you what, Mom," John said trying to convince his mother "If we fall into something like this again, we promise to back out."

"What if you aren't as lucky the next time you're in some trouble?" Mrs. Martin asked still not impressed.

"We promise we won't be in any serious trouble, Mom," Joe said reassuringly "We can't back off now."

"Joe's right," John added "We can't back off and let those goons go after they tried to kill Joe and Jeff. We should get our hands on them."

The idea of provocation seemed to work as Mrs. Martin thought for some time about what her boys had said.

"Ok," she said finally "I will leave this to your father. What he says will be final."

Later, the family talked on the same subject over dinner. Mr. Martin was not wanting to let his boys go towards any more danger but John and Joe used the same technique they had used earlier to convince their mother, and it seemed to work with their father as well. Mr. Martin agreed to John and Joe's request of letting them continue with the case on the condition that they would be extremely careful. Earlier, Joe and Jeff had taken a taxi to 24 Carat before dinner to fetch their bikes.

After dinner, Joe called up Mr. Bucks to tell them about the day's happenings.

"I am extremely sorry to hear that," he said worried that the men tried to kill Joe and Jeff "You're free to back off if you want. I don't want anything to happen to you guys, you see."

"It's ok, Mr. Bucks," Joe said reassuringly "We will move ahead with the case. In fact, we have an advantage I think, because the thieves won't be expecting us anytime soon."

"Ok then," Mr. Bucks replied "It's your wish. Just take care."

"Goodnight, Mr. Bucks," Joe wished as he put down the receiver.

"Did the eavesdropper pay us a visit today?" Joe asked as he entered the bedroom where John was already on his bed.

"No," John replied "Not today. He was too preoccupied with you guys, I suppose."

"They even took our wallets and cell phones," Joe revealed.

"We will get them back once we catch them," John assured "You can use my old cell phone for the time being. I have an old SIM card as well. I will search for it tomorrow morning."

"Sounds cool," Joe agreed "Well, Goodnight, brother. I am too tired."

"Goodnight!"

"John! Joe!" someone called out knocking on the bedroom door.

John woke up at once and getting down from the bed, checked the time on the table clock. It read 00:20 hours. He then went up to the door and opened it to find Mr. Martin standing outside.

"What happened, Dad?" John asked puzzled at the fact that he was calling them at midnight.

"Mr. Buck's on the phone," Mr. Oswald Martin replied feeling pretty sleepy himself "He wants to talk to you. He seems tensed."

John rushed down the stairs and into the hall and within moments, picked up the receiver.

"Hello!" he greeted "John Martin speaking."

"John, it's me, Jean Bucks," a worried and excited voice said from the other end "I have news for you."

"What is it, Mr. Bucks?" John asked.

"Well, you need to come over right now," Mr. Bucks said.

"But why? What happened?"

"There are three men in my backyard," Mr. Bucks explained "They have shovels and some other equipment as well. And they have been digging all over my backyard for quite a few minutes now. I suspect those are the thieves and they have come to get the second pot of treasure as well."

7
Let's Go Trekking

* * *

"We will come right over, Mr. Bucks," John said as he kept the receiver down. He knew this was an incredibly genuine chance to catch the thieves in their actions.

"What happened?" Mr. Martin asked. He was standing at the stairs curious to know why the boys' client had called this late at night.

"The thieves are presently trying to dig out the second pot of treasure, Dad," John replied as he rushed towards the stairs "Joe and I will have to leave right away."

"Well, take care," Mr. Martin called out as John entered his bedroom.

John shook Joe awake and told him about Mr. Bucks' call and its purpose.

"We should leave right away," Joe said getting out of the bed.

"Right," John replied "Oh! I forgot to call Jeff. I will call him right away."

John dialed the number to Jeff's residence from his cell phone. Their Uncle answered it after the phone rang for quite some time.

"Hello, Uncle Walter," John greeted "Can I talk to Jeff? It's urgent."

"Oh ok," the Uncle said.

After about a minute someone picked up the receiver.

"Hello?" a sleepy voice answered.

"Jeff, John here. Get ready quickly. We need to go to Mr. Bucks' home."

"Why? What happened?" Jeff asked yawning.

"The thieves are trying to dig the second pot of treasure out. Mr. Bucks called and said so just now. There's no time to waste. Get ready as soon as possible."

"Right," Jeff replied waking up completely hearing the news "Will be ready in a jiffy."

The two Martins got ready and bid goodnight to their parents who told them to be very careful in reply. They then walked out of the house as Mr. Martin closed the door behind them. A chilling wind blew in the air making the boys shiver.

"It's too cold," Joe said as he rubbed his arms trying to keep himself warm.

"I haven't been out at this time of the night in a long time now," John replied recalling the last time they were out at midnight which was when they were solving another case.

They were after a gang of criminals who were planning to murder two soccer players during their visit to Fischerberg City for a match. The three Js, back then, had been out at midnight to keep a watch at the goons. That case had given them a lot of fame and the two soccer stars even gave them an autographed jersey each for their bravery.

Presently, though, John and Joe took out their motorcycles from the garage and started them. They got onto their bikes and went to Jeff's home where they found Jeff starting his bike.

"It has very little fuel," Jeff said as he saw his cousin brothers stopping their motorbikes on the road at the front of the house "Will we have time to refuel it?"

"No," John replied "We need to hurry. Leave your bike at your garage and hop onto my bike behind me."

Jeff did as told and soon the three were on their way to Mr. Bucks' house roaring off into the silent night.

Fischerberg City was very lively during the daytime. Grown-ups went to work, kids went to schools, and shopkeepers opened their shops just like any other city. It had a vibrant night life as well with a variety of dining restaurants, clubs, bars and discos spread across it. However, the city went to sleep by midnight and there was minimal traffic on the roads with most of it being taxis carrying passengers going to or coming from the airport. Even the traffic lights blinked only the yellow light, unlike the daytime when it worked in its usual manner. The city would start to come back to life by around 5 in the morning but presently it was pretty silent all around.

It took only a little more than twenty minutes for the boys to reach Mr. Bucks' place as compared to the usual forty minutes, which the journey took, in the day time. As the boys approached the house, they saw a van parked right at the front of the house. John signaled Joe to stop. Both the bikes came to a halt and switched off their head lights.

"The thieves are still there," John pointed out.

"Do we go and nab them?" Joe asked.

"I think so," Jeff replied, "For all we know, even Mr. Bucks might be in trouble."

"You're right," Joe agreed "Let's go."

But before the boys could start their bikes, they saw three men emerge out of Mr. Bucks' compound and walk rapidly towards the van. The three Js stood where they were, looking at what the men were doing. They even noticed a man holding something round with both his hands and the others holding some digging equipment.

"That man must be holding the pot," Jeff whispered.

"Could be," John replied in a whisper "Where is Mr. Bucks, though? Still looking from the windows?"

"I think he is in some kind of trouble," Joe figured "He doesn't seem to be like the man who would silently watch the treasure, which his family and ancestors had so well protected, being stolen away."

"You could be right," the other two said in agreement.

As the boys talked, the van started and its headlight turned on. Soon enough, it started to move in the opposite direction to where the three boys were.

"Jeff, take Joe's bike and go to Mr. Bucks' house," John instructed quickly "He might be in some trouble and may need help. Joe, get off your bike and hop on behind me. We will follow the van."

Joe got off from his bike, handed the keys to Jeff and got onto John's motorcycle in the back seat. Soon John and Joe were off following the van.

The van went north for quite some time. John didn't turn on his headlights on purpose so as not to warn the thieves. He knew that if any Police patrol car spotted them, they would be in trouble for riding the bike at night with the headlights turned off, but he was willing to risk it. A few cars zoomed by on the road as they followed the van. Every time John and Joe spotted a pair of lights approaching, they prayed to God for it to not be a Police car and every time God seemed to listen to their prayers as it turned out to be a taxi or a private vehicle.

The journey went on for around ten minutes and then the van slowed down once they were in the middle of the Midlands Forest. John slowed down his bike as well. The van maneuvered a little towards the right and stopped at the roadside with its parking lights turned on. John followed the suit and brought his motorcycle to a halt on the roadside about two hundred meters away.

They spotted three men get down from the van with one of them holding something which looked like the pot they had stolen from Mr. Bucks' backyard. The three men walked towards the right and went into the forest. The boys went up to the van and silently and carefully checked if there was anyone inside. They got a negative result. Joe checked if the doors were unlocked so that they could get in and check the van. They might get some clues as to who these men were. But the doors were locked as well. John spotted the faint trail the men had followed and signaled Joe to follow him as they went into the forest following the trail.

The night was unusually silent with the occasional sounds of the tree branches rubbing against each other in the breeze or that of the night insects. The cold breeze made the boys shiver with cold. It was even colder in the middle of the forest than they had felt when they had walked out of their house. The boys heard the sound of shoes stepping on a broken branch or trampling on the grasses in the distance. Carefully matching their footsteps with the sounds so as not to arouse the thieves' suspicion, they moved ahead towards the direction from where the sound came. The boys tried to gain up a little on the thieves so as to listen to anything that the men might talk about.

Carefully taking strides, the boys gained a few meters on the men, enough to hear the men whispering among them. But they still couldn't make out what the men were talking about and hence, the brothers tried to get a little closer.

"Is it really necessary to hide it here?" one of them was whispering.

"It is," another voice whispered in reply "We will take it to that 24 Carat shop later."

John and Joe exchanged glances at the mention of the shop's name. As they did so, John accidentally stepped on a broken twig on the ground sending a low cracking sound into the silent forest night. The boys stopped in their tracks.

"Did you hear that sound?" a third voice among the thieves asked as they stopped as well "It seemed to come from behind us."

"No, I didn't," replied one of them.

The brothers decided not to risk it and blow their cover up and hence decided to drop back a little from the thieves.

The footsteps of the three men got further away but the boys made their stride carefully and perfectly in unison with them. Joe looked up at the night sky and saw the moon brightly shining and lighting their path up to a certain extent. It was a half-moon with a few stars scattered here and there in the sky. The cold breeze was becoming stronger and it made the leaves rustle among them and branches scratch among each other. All these sounds made it a little difficult for the boys to listen to the footsteps.

"Are there any wild animals here?" Joe asked starting to feel a little scared.

"I don't know," John replied who himself had started to feel a bit worried as to where they were headed to.

The trail got fainter and fainter presently, and it wasn't long before it completely vanished. Suddenly the footsteps stopped. The boys stopped as well.

"They must have stopped to do something," John assumed.

"Probably," Joe replied "We will wait for them to start moving again.

John pulled out his cell phone and checked the time. It was a little past one-thirty.

"I wonder how Mr. Bucks and Jeff are," Joe

wondered out in a whisper.

"They should be fine," John stated.

"I was expecting a message or a call from him by now."

"Nah, that isn't possible," John informed "There's no network coverage here in the middle of this forest. We won't receive any calls or texts anyway."

The boys waited for some thirty minutes but the footsteps didn't resume. All that the boys could hear were the natural sounds of the forest.

"Should we move up a little," John asked, "It's difficult to listen to the footsteps among these sounds."

"True," Joe agreed as the boys moved up a little towards where the last sound of the footsteps had come from hoping to catch any sound that the men might make.

They went on for a few meters but didn't hear anything. So they walked up almost a hundred meters but they still couldn't catch any sound. A few more meters and it still yielded no results. Finally, the boys stopped in their tracks and John said with a worried look,

"I think we are lost!"

8

Threat for Mr. Bucks

❄ ❄ ❄

In the meantime, Jeff rode on Joe's motorcycle to reach their client's house. He parked the bike in the driveway of the house, ran up to the door and rang the doorbell and waited for a few seconds. However, there was no reply. He rang the doorbell again but again no one came to open the door.

"Mr. Bucks!" Jeff called out from the main door assuming that Mr. Bucks must have thought it was the thieves who were ringing the doorbell trying to get into the house and capture him "It's Jeff Martin!"

Jeff knew by now that these thieves could do anything in order to successfully steal the treasure and hence, had started to feel a little anxious. At the start of the case, the boys had assumed that these were just some petty thieves trying to earn a lifetime's amount by selling off the treasure. But throughout the course of the investigation and thanks to everything that the boys had faced, including the threatening notes, the hit on the head and getting trapped in a shed with leaking gas coming from a cylinder whose knob had been broken on purpose, they had been forced to believe that these thieves were no ordinary. They could go to any extent to successfully carry out their mission and could even kill if someone came in between. However, whether they had any guns with them was something the boys had still not figured out. It seemed more likely that they didn't own any because had they owned them, they could have easily shot Joe and Jeff dead, but again they couldn't rule anything out, not with this gang of thieves. Also, had they been shot, that would have made the case more serious and the Police would have gotten on their trail. But their idea of blowing them up with the shed courtesy of the leaking gas and making the whole incident look like an accident made more sense as that would render the thieves safe.

Questions like these were unanswered so far and the boys didn't have enough clues to get to the answer of them. For instance, how did the thieves find out that Mr. Bucks owned a treasure if that was a well-kept family secret as their client had told them to be? Another instance was that the thieves knew the pinpoint location of the first pot of treasure because when the boys visited Mr. Bucks' backyard, they could see that the whole backyard had only one pit. Had they not known the exact location, the whole backyard would have been dug out in order to find the pot. Also, how come Mr. Bucks did not hear anything when the first pot was being dug out, unlike now, when he had heard the second pot being dug out and hence, had warned the boys and told them to come over? According to the man, he had only discovered the theft the next morning.

All these questions could be answered only by Mr. Jean Bucks and Jeff decided to ask him all of these and hoped to get a few answers once he met their client.

However, there were other questions as well which were unanswered and which Jeff knew couldn't be answered by Mr. Bucks. For example, who did the house with the shed where the boys were trapped belong to? Also, how big was the gang of thieves they were after? Earlier they had thought it to be two because Mr. Dillon Johnson from the 24 Carat shop had stated that two men had come with the stolen treasure, but today they saw three men getting into the van which John and Joe had gone following. A large gang of thieves would be too difficult for the boys to handle. Also, the larger the gang, the more dangerous it gets.

Presently, though, Jeff stood at the main door continuously ringing the doorbell without getting any answer from the other side. A chill ran down his spine as he realized Mr. Bucks could be in trouble. The men might have tied him up and left him to die just like they had done with him and Joe earlier. Jeff also didn't rule out the possibility of the thieves kidnapping Jean Bucks and keeping him somewhere till the entire loot was converted into money. But then Jeff remembered that they had seen only three men walking out of Mr. Bucks' compound and getting into the van a few minutes back, and surely, none of those three men looked like their client.

"Mr. Bucks!" Jeff called out loudly, this time banging on the door with his fist, but still got no reply.

Then it struck upon Jeff to go around the house and onto the backyard. Maybe Mr. Bucks was in his backyard. Even the back door might be open and if that was the case indeed, he could go into the house through it.

Jeff ran towards the right of the house. The grasses were neatly chopped off at first but then, towards the latter part of the front yard, the grasses were tall and weeds grew all around. It was surely not possible for one single man to maintain the whole house, Jeff thought. It was dark and Jeff realized that he had no torch with him.

'Drat! Those men stole my cell phone as well,' he cursed in his thought. If he still had his cell phone with him, he could have used the flashlight of it to guide his path, but presently, all he had to himself was the faint moonlight.

At least he was lucky in the aspect that it was a clear sky that day. Had it been cloudy, the moon would have hidden behind the clouds giving him no light at all.

Jeff carefully took his steps over the tall grass and weeds. He feared there might be snakes around and hence, had to be extremely cautious. He reached the corner of the house and turned left from there. The path was no different in this part as well. In fact, the grasses only grew taller. Mosquitoes surrounded him and bit him everywhere from his hands to his face. Jeff tried to chase them away but there were a lot of them and if he chased one away, another came from the other side and bit him. He kept scratching himself till he finally reached the back of the house.

The scene he saw was something Jeff hadn't expected so far. There were multiple pits in the backyard mostly concentrated towards the southern part of the compound. He ran over to the location crossing the small kitchen garden on his way. There were at least some eight or nine pits, all dug to a depth of around two to three feet just like the pit the thieves had dug out to steal the first pot. Jeff was still wondering whether there were so many pots of treasure or was it that the thieves didn't know the exact location of the second pot, when his eyes fell on something on the ground, beside the pit he was closest to, shining in the moonlight. He bent down and picked it up. On looking at it carefully, he realized it was the same chocolate wrapper, with the words 'Sweet-O' on it, just like the one they had found in the pit on the first day and also the one Mrs. Martin had found near their kitchen door.

'So sweet tooth was here as well,' Jeff assumed to himself.

However, he still found no trace of Mr. Bucks anywhere. He figured he might be inside his home tied up or maybe unconscious. The thieves might have tried to get him out of the way for at least some time so that they could carry out their digging in peace. There was also the probability that the thieves might have found out that Mr. Bucks had warned the three Js and hence, they did something bad to him. Jeff just hoped, though, that Mr. Bucks wasn't in any serious trouble.

He started walking towards the back door of the house. A few seconds later, he noticed a dark figure lying near the steps of the back porch. Jeff jogged up to the figure and looked at it. It was indeed Mr. Jean Bucks. He seemed to be out cold.

'The thieves must have hit him,' Jeff assumed.

However, just to be sure that things weren't more serious, Jeff tried to feel for the man's pulse on his neck. He soon heaved a sigh of relief as he found the pulse still beating.

Jeff rushed toward the back door of the house and found it ajar. He went in and looked for the kitchen. Within moments, he came out of the house with a glass of water and sprinkled it on Mr. Bucks' face.

"Mr. Bucks, wake up!" Jeff called out shaking their client's body.

He noticed the man's right fist was closed appearing as if he had something in it. Jeff opened the fist and found a piece of paper there. He took it and put it in his jeans pocket for the time being.

Then he sprinkled some more water on Mr. Bucks' face and finally his eyelids fluttered as the man came to his senses. He moaned with pain and felt for the back of his head.

"Mr. Bucks," Jeff called out "Are you alright?"

"Uh, yes," the man said with a quivering voice "I will be alright, I guess."

Jeff helped Mr. Bucks get up onto his feet and the two slowly walked into the house and into the dining room. Mr. Bucks fetched himself a glass of water and gulped it down. He then sat across Jeff on one of the chairs.

"Thank You, Jeff," he said starting to feel better.

"But what actually happened, Mr. Bucks?" Jeff asked impatiently, eager to know what had happened.

"Uh," Jean Bucks started "I was sleeping when I heard some sounds coming from my backyard. I got up from the bed and looked from one of the windows to see three men digging out soil quite rapidly in there. So I called up John and told him to come right over. Then I went back to the window to see what they were up to. They were still digging but now at a different spot. It seemed like they didn't know the location of the second pot. They just knew that it was somewhere towards the southern part of the backyard and hence, were digging all over my backyard towards the south."

"Yeah, I assumed that," Jeff said adding on that he had seen almost ten pits in the backyard.

"Yeah," Mr. Bucks said nodding his head "I was quite happy with the fact they were digging in the wrong locations every time. I guessed you guys would reach and catch them before they got to the correct location. So I just decided to watch them until the time you arrived. But that wasn't the case, unfortunately. They soon started digging at the exact location where the pot was. I was horror stricken. I had to do something or they would have taken my pot and I would have stood there watching them steal it. But I didn't know what to do. My brain wasn't working then. I just went out of the back door and shouted at them to stop. The men were surprised at first but then realized that they were three and I was only one. Though I was scared a little, I stood there. I wanted to give them some resistance at least. The three walked up to me and one of them punched me. I gave him one back. I tried to fight them but they soon overpowered me and then something hit me on the back of my head and I don't remember anything from then until you found me."

"I see," Jeff said and then he remembered, "Oh, I found this piece of paper in your fist."

Jeff pulled out the paper and unfolded it. Then he read out loud what was written on it.

'*That's for you. Thank you for bringing the three Js into this. We will get to you once we are done with our main priorities.*'

"They must have put the paper in my fist after they knocked me out," Mr. Bucks suggested.

"The font style and size are the same as the ones in the threatening notes we received," Jeff observed, "It has to be the thieves who put this in your fist."

"Yes," Mr. Bucks agreed "So that is supposed to mean as a threat to me?"

"Right, but only after they are done with their main priorities," Jeff pointed out.

"What is that supposed to mean?" Mr. Bucks asked.

"I guess after they are done selling off the entire treasure," Jeff replied.

"I won't let them do that," Mr. Bucks replied rather enraged that the thieves managed to steal both the pots of treasure.

"Cool down, Mr. Bucks," Jeff assured "We will catch those thieves soon and recover your treasure. John and Joe are presently following those three men."

"Great!" Mr. Bucks said rather relieved upon hearing this "Did you get any updates from them?"

"Not yet," Jeff replied shaking his head sideways "I will call John up and ask."

Jeff asked for the telephone to which Mr. Bucks took him to the hall. The three boys remembered each other's telephone numbers for cases of emergencies like these and it proved quite useful at the present. Jeff dialed John's number but a voice from the other side said that the number was not reachable at present. He tried again but got the same response.

"It's not reachable," Jeff said hoping that his brothers were not in some serious danger.

"Oh!" Mr. Bucks replied with a glum face.

Jeff could see that their client was pretty shaken up by the night's happenings including the fact that the second pot of treasure, which he had hidden and protected so well, was stolen too. He wanted to ask him about how the thieves came to know that he owned two pots of treasure but decided that it would be better to take his leave at the moment and come again the next day with John and Joe.

"You rest now, Mr. Bucks," Jeff said, "I will take your leave. We will pay you a visit tomorrow."

"Ok, sure," Jean Bucks said as he said goodnight to Jeff.

Jeff got out of the house and got onto Joe's bike and sped away. The whole happenings of the night had puzzled Jeff even more. If the thieves knew the exact location of the first pot, then how come they didn't know the location of the second pot? Also, why did the thieves go towards Portville? Did they live there? Was the gang's hideout in Portville?

There were too many loose ends at present and Jeff decided that the three would have to sit together and discuss the case for them to make any breakthrough.

9

A Scary Night Results in a Lucky Day

* * *

Jeff parked the motorcycle inside their garage and rang the doorbell. His father opened the door after a few moments.

"Jeff," he said, "Why did Mr. Bucks call you guys?"

Jeff told his father and mother, who had come out of the bedroom by now, everything as he walked into the hall and closed the main door behind him.

"That's sad," Mrs. Claudia Martin said once his son was over debriefing them "Mr. Bucks must be so dejected."

"He is," Jeff replied, "We will pay him a visit tomorrow."

"So John and Joe are still not back?" Walter Martin asked a little worried about his nephews.

"I don't think so," Jeff replied, "I will try calling John again."

Jeff walked up to the landline telephone and dialed John's number. But he got the same response that the number was not reachable.

"Maybe there's some problem with the network," Mr. Martin suggested, "Call up their residence and ask if they have returned."

"I don't think they have returned," Jeff said thinking "Had they been back from the chase, they would have called up here to find if I had come back. Plus, I don't think they would have returned home directly. They would have stopped at Mr. Bucks' house on the way and if that was the case, they would have surely called here once they found out from Mr. Bucks that I have returned."

"It's true, though," his mother agreed.

"So if I call up their home and ask, Uncle Oswald and Aunt Helena would just get worried," Jeff pointed out.

"But what if they are really in danger?" Mr. Walter Martin asked still a little worried.

Jeff shrugged.

"They must be on the thieves' trail," Claudia said soothingly "Let's wait until tomorrow morning. If they don't return by then, then we will assume that they are in danger."

The other two agreed to this and soon went to their respective rooms to catch some sleep.

"Where did the three of them go?" Joe asked still pondering "We didn't hear them leaving."

"We must have lost the sound in the middle of the forest's sounds," John presumed.

John took out his cell phone and switched on the flashlight. They were stranded in the Midlands Forest and were surrounded by tall trees and certain insects. The branches of the trees went high and covered the top to such an extent that even the moonlight didn't reach them properly at times. They had come really deep into the forest following the thieves and now they sensed that they were lost.

"Let's move towards the direction from where we

came," Joe advised.

"Ok," John agreed "But I don't remember properly where we came from."

Joe realized that his brother was right. They had taken a lot of bends and turns while following the men and now both of them didn't remember properly the exact route they had followed.

"Do your phone have a magnetic compass?" Joe asked "The highway is towards the west. So we can follow that direction maybe."

"That idea came to my mind as well," John said rather glumly "But no, I don't have a compass on my phone."

The boys were stranded in the middle of the forest with no sense of direction at all. They had no idea which way to move. They tried to retrace their route by looking at the overturned grass but after some time, that stopped yielding results as well. The boys had come trekking in these forests once, some three years back, but they hadn't come this deep back then. The forest reportedly had wild animals in it but John and Joe were lucky that they hadn't encountered one so far.

"I miss Jeff," John said, "Had he been with us now, we would have been out of the forest soon."

"Couldn't agree with you more," Joe said agreeing to what his brother said.

The boys' cousin, Jeff Martin had a very good sense of directions. He could tell the directions accurately by just looking at the moon or the stars. Had he been with John and Joe today, they would have been on their way out at the moment.

"I wonder how Mr. Bucks is," Joe wondered out loud. The thought of Jeff made him remember that he had gone to check in on their client.

"Let's think about Mr. Bucks later," John said starting to get a little scared "Let's think about our escape for the moment."

"You're right," Joe said rather sheepishly.

The boys thought for a few moments but couldn't come up with anything. It was around 3 am now and the forest looked scarier than ever. The boys suddenly heard a howling sound.

"What's that?" Joe asked startled.

"A wolf," John replied scared "Keep quiet. The sound came from quite far away."

The two kept silent for a few minutes to see if they could hear the howl again but it was negative.

"The wolf must have gone towards the other direction," Joe assumed.

"Could be," John agreed.

"I guess, we have to wait here till sunrise," Joe said regretfully as he sat down on the forest floor "We can look at the sun and figure out the direction then."

"I was thinking the same thing," John replied sitting down across Joe "Besides, we may only get further into the forest if we keep moving randomly."

"True," Joe agreed "I just hope we don't encounter any animals."

They heard a shrieking sound just then and something moving near the boys.

"What's that!" the boys jumped up in surprise.

A mouse, scared by the boys' sudden jump, ran away towards the dense shrubs.

"Only a mouse," replied John sitting down again.

The boys sat there and tried to listen to every sound that they could to be careful about any wild animals that might be approaching. Neither of them could afford a moment of a break from their listening duty. The boys loved trekking and camping a lot, but this experience was surely not lovable. The forest, which was a favorite spot for the nature lovers, looked like a dangerous haunted place at night. Seconds passed into minutes and minutes into hours.

Soon, the boys saw the first rays of the sun at daybreak.

"There's the sun!" John exclaimed "That means east is towards that direction. We have to go west."

"Let's not lose any more time," Joe replied getting up onto his feet.

The two started moving westwards. The path didn't seem any more familiar but they kept moving nonetheless. Eager to get out of the forest as quickly as possible, they took long and fast-paced strides. They had no idea on how far they had come in and hence, didn't even have an approximate guess as to how much time they would need to get out of the forest.

"Hey, look over there," John said suddenly stopping in his tracks.

Joe turned to John and saw him pointing towards their right.

"What's there?" Joe asked not seeing anything extraordinary. All he could see were trees and bushes.

"The trees over there seems to be less dense than in here," John pointed out.

Joe looked carefully and realized that John was indeed correct.

"Is that the exit?" Joe guessed.

"Let's go and see for ourselves," John replied.

The two went towards their right. As they marched on, the trees started becoming less dense and within moments, they crossed the trees and reached a large opening in the middle of the forest that was spread out in a rather circular shape.

The boys stood there stunned.

"Why are there no trees here?" John wondered out loud.

"Beats me," Joe replied equally puzzled.

They walked over to the opening and looked around to see if there were any marks of burnt grass or firewood. That would have confirmed that there were campers here who had cleared up the shrubs and trees to camp there.

"I don't think campers would cut down trees, though," John said replying to Joe's suggestion that the place was used as a campsite.

"You are right," he accepted "But what is this place then?"

"It sure is rather extraordinary to find an opening like this in the middle of this dense forest."

"Look over here," Joe said suddenly calling John over.

"What did you find?" John asked walking up to his brother.

Presently, Joe crouched down and pointed at an area in the ground.

"The entire area is covered with grass except for this portion," he pointed out.

"You're right," John said looking at the portion Joe was pointing at.

It was a rather circular area of about a meter in diameter in the middle of the entire opening.

"It looks like this area was dug out recently and then the soil was put back," John said with his mind racing.

"We should dig this area out to see if there's anything under the soil here," Joe suggested.

"Agreed," John replied.

The two boys tried to dig out the soil with their bare hands as they had no digging equipment with them. It took them quite a few moments and a lot of labor work to finally arrive at something.

"There's something here," John declared.

The two cleared the soil around the thing and

brought out a plastic pot from the pit. John uncovered the lid to see what it contained.

"Whoa!" he exclaimed with surprise "This is nothing but Mr. Bucks' stolen treasure!"

10
Suspect Identified!

❄ ❄ ❄

"What a find!" Joe exclaimed as he saw the treasure.

The pot as filled with ancient jewelry, gold bars, gold coins and precious stones with ancient Romanian inscriptions on the gold coins dated back to the nineteenth century. The boys picked a few of the treasures and held it in their hands.

"I am holding a treasure for the first time," John said feeling elated.

"I am seeing one for the first time," Joe said equally excited.

"No wonder the thieves were after these precious things," John pointed out.

"So this is where the thieves were heading to yesterday," Joe said realizing that the thieves came into the forest to hide the treasure there.

"But did they actually make this entire opening in the forest just for the sake of hiding a treasure?" John asked puzzled.

"There is certainly more to this opening than just hiding this pot," Joe said thinking hard "But I don't know what."

"We will soon find that out, I guess," John said as he put the treasure in his hand back into the pot "We should take this pot back with us."

"We certainly should," Joe replied putting the contents of his hand back into the pot as well.

John put the lid back on the opening of the pot and picked it up. Holding it tightly and carefully, the boys moved back into the forest away from the opening.

"We must continue on our way to move west then," Joe said as the boys resumed their quest to escape the forest.

It was almost around 7 in the morning now and the boys knew their parents would start getting worried as they were missing. They quickened their pace as they wanted to avoid any steps that their parents or Jeff and his family might take once they assumed that they had gone missing. They might call the police to file a missing person report. But the boys knew it well that if the cops were brought in on this, then they would find out all about the treasure and thus, the mission would be a failure.

Within a few more minutes, the boys saw the trees getting less dense. They could hear the noise of the traffic in the distance.

"I can hear the highway," John said getting excited.

"Same here," Joe said.

The boys felt a sudden burst of energy in them and they almost jogged towards the direction of the sound of the traffic. It wasn't like they didn't want to run, though. They wanted to, but the shrubs and overhanging branches of the trees made it impossible for them to do so. They had to carefully dodge the branches and thorns of some of the plants and trees to make their way.

Soon enough, they reached the edge of the forest.

"Uh, heaven!" Joe said relieved.

"I will call up home and tell them we are going back," John said taking out his phone which was almost discharged by now courtesy to the excessive use of the flashlight back in the forest during the night.

As John made the call home, Joe looked around to see in which part of the highway they were. They had parked the bike some ten kilometers away from Fischerberg City and the location where they were standing at the moment sure didn't look like the one where they had parked the bike.

"I think we are closer to Portville," Joe said once John was done with the phone call.

"Yeah," John agreed "Let's walk towards Fischerberg."

The pot of treasure changed places by shifting from John's hands to Joe's hands as the boys started walking south towards Fischerberg.

"Do you think we should stop by at Mr. Bucks' place and return the treasure?" Joe asked his elder brother.

"Not right now," John replied "I want to ask him a couple of questions later. That is after I take a shower and take some rest. We will return the pot at the same time."

There were certainly a lot of unanswered questions in the case so far and the boys would certainly have to meet their client to see if they could get any answers. They decided they would get home, freshen up and take some rest until lunch time. They would visit Mr. Bucks after lunch.

After walking for about twenty minutes, the boys reached the location from where they had entered the forest. The bike was there, parked as it was in the previous night. John started it and with Joe on the backseat, sped off towards home.

As John was parking the bike in the garage, the front door opened and Mr. Oswald Martin, his wife, and

Jeff rushed out.

"Where were you two?" Mrs. Martin asked considerately.

"Let us get in first, at least," Joe said with a small laugh.

The five sat down at the hall with John and Joe being in the spotlight. They narrated the incidents and told the audience about following the thieves into the forest, losing their way and finally finding the pot of treasure. The Martins' parents and Jeff listened to their story with awe and a lot of interest. John opened the lid of the pot after they were done with their explanation much to the excitement of the others.

"Wow!" the three exclaimed.

"We were lucky to come upon this pot accidentally," Joe said, "But this is quite a find."

"Obviously it is," Jeff agreed "Mr. Bucks will be very happy to see it."

"We will go to his place after lunch and return it," John said.

"Right," Jeff agreed "You guys rest now."

Jeff said goodbye to them and took his leave. Mr. Martin went to his bedroom to get ready for work and Mrs. Helena Martin went to the kitchen to prepare breakfast. John and Joe went upstairs to their room to freshen up and get into fresh clothes.

Later, they went downstairs for a breakfast of Bacon, eggs, and milk.

"So what are you guys going to do next?" the boys' mother asked sitting across them on the dining table. She already had her breakfast with her husband who had left for work by the time the boys were done freshening up.

"We will go return the pot in the afternoon," John replied, "We also have to ask Mr. Bucks a few questions."

"Will he be home then?" their mother asked.

"Yeah," Joe replied "I called him up a few moments ago to ask about his availability and he said he has taken a leave today from his office because of yesterday night's happenings. I don't know what happened yesterday night, though."

"We will have to ask Jeff about it," John recommended "I guess the three of us should discuss the case in the afternoon after lunch for some time. We will go meet Mr. Bucks after that."

"Suits me fine," Joe agreed.

"But right now, you guys should finish the breakfast and get some sleep," Mrs. Martin advised to which the boys agreed.

They soon finished their breakfast and went upstairs to their room to catch some sleep.

Jeff arrived shortly after John and Joe were done with lunch. He was expecting that they would go to Mr. Bucks' house but when John told him that they needed to discuss the case first, he went upstairs to the boys' bedroom.

"Tell us what happened yesterday night after we left to follow the van," John asked Jeff as he laid down relaxing on the bed.

"Oh yes," Jeff replied, "I had almost forgotten to tell you guys."

He told his brothers everything about the incidents of the previous night from the existence of multiple pits in the backyard to finding a knocked out Jean Bucks. He also told them about the threatening letter he had found in Mr. Bucks' fist. John and Joe listened to their cousin with attention and curiosity.

"So Mr. Bucks heard sounds coming from the backyard when they were digging out the second pot but nothing when they were trying to steal the first pot?" Joe wondered with a puzzled expression on his face.

"Exactly," Jeff replied, "That's what confuses me as

well."

"Also, another thing to note is that the men dug out at several locations trying to find the second pot unlike the first," John pointed out.

"Yeah," Jeff agreed "all the pits were concentrated towards the southern part of the backyard, though."

"And the pit for the first pot was on the northern side of the backyard," John said.

"Correct," Joe replied, "But what has always baffled me is that the thieves knew the exact location of the first pot."

"But didn't know the exact location of the second pot," Jeff added.

"Yes," John replied nodding his head "There has to be someone who knew about the treasure apart from Mr. Bucks' family."

"There certainly has to be," Joe replied "There's no doubt about it. Someone wouldn't randomly go to some backyard hoping to find treasure there."

"But the confusion is that if the thieves indeed knew the location of the first treasure, then why wasn't it the same for the second pot?" Jeff reiterated.

"Beats me," John replied.

"Me too," Joe said shrugging.

"There is another thing that I want to get an answer to," Jeff said "And it's not related to Mr. Bucks. Who did the house in the shed of which I and Joe were locked up belong to?"

"Oh yes," Joe replied "I had almost forgotten about that shed."

"We will have to find that out," John said thinking "But how?"

"Ask nearby people?" Jeff suggested.

"I guess, we could do that when we go to Mr. Bucks' house," John said, "We will have to take a detour for that, though."

The shed where the boys were kept was in North-west Fischerberg, which was towards the west of Yorkville where the boys lived. Mr. Bucks' house was in St. Bryan's which was towards the north eastern side of Fischerberg, unlike Yorkville which was towards the west. However, North-west Fischerberg was quite close to the boys' home and hence, it wouldn't be much of an inconvenience to get there.

"Coming to our incidents," Joe said, "I still don't get why they hid the pot in the jungle."

"To hide it away for a few days, obviously," Jeff suggested.

"But they had taken the treasure of the first pot to 24 Carat shop instead of hiding the whole pot there," Joe countered.

"As you mention 24 Carat, I remember listening to them talking about taking the second pot of treasure to that shop later," John said remembering what he had overheard as they were following the men before they were lost "But why to the same shop where they knew that the manager had been alerted by us that those gold and jewels were stolen loot?"

"Correct," Joe replied, "That puzzles me as well."

"Also, I remember you guys said about the big opening in the middle of the forest," Jeff pointed out "What's that opening for?"

"No idea," Joe replied, "But could the first pot of treasure be hidden under the soil in that opening as well, like the second pot?"

"Could be," John replied thinking hard "But we can't go there and dig out the whole opening, can we?"

"Certainly not," Jeff replied "We will have to go back there and look for clues."

"Agreed," Joe said in agreement and then pointed

out, “But we don’t know the exact location of that opening. We were lost at that time, you see.”

“I know a Mr. Hal Harper who flies a private helicopter from the airport, taking people to their destinations,” Jeff notified, “We could take his help.”

“That’s great,” John replied excited at the idea “How well do you know him?”

“He is a college friend of my Dad,” Jeff replied, “So yeah, I know him pretty well.”

“Awesome,” John said “We will carry out this plan tomorrow morning then.”

“That’s fine,” Joe said “But all this brainstorming has yielded very little answers. This case is going over my head.”

“Let’s go to Mr. Bucks’ house now,” Jeff suggested, “We might get some answers there.”

The boys first went to North-west Fischerberg and asked people they could find near the house as to who it belonged to. A lot of them didn’t know anything about it. However, some fifteen minutes of asking led to some positive results. A person who seemed to live nearby and was taking his black Alsatian out for a walk told them that the house belonged to a Mr. Oleson who was a rich businessman. He added that he didn’t live there anymore and had shifted to the Middle East with his family some three or four years back.

Satisfied with the answer, the boys headed for Mr. Bucks’ house.

“Do you think Mr. Oleson is involved in this?” Joe asked looking at John from over his bike.

“Not sure,” John replied over the sound of the engine “He is a rich businessman, though. So I don’t think he would be interested in stealing stuff like that.”

The three soon arrived at Mr. Bucks’ mansion. They parked their bikes in the driveway and went up onto the front porch. Jeff rang the doorbell. Within moments, Jean Bucks opened the door.

"Hello, boys," Mr. Bucks greeted in his usual husky voice as he opened the door "Come in."

Even though he invited the boys in with a smile on his face, the boys could make out that he was actually rather glum. He wasn't his usual self and seemed a bit preoccupied. He didn't even notice the pot of treasure that Joe was holding. It wasn't like Mr. Bucks joked and danced around in his usual self, though. He was a pretty sober person, as the boys had seen him, but presently, he looked sad and depressed, preoccupied with the fact that both of his treasure pots were stolen.

But as soon as he saw Joe handing him the pot of treasure, his face brightened.

"Where did you get this?" he asked excited and cheered up.

The boys explained their story and how they had come upon the hidden pot in the forest as they sat in the hall of Mr. Buck's big house.

"It's really good work from you," he said congratulating the boys after they were all seated.

"Thank you, sir," John said not revealing the real purpose of their visit right away.

"I am indeed impressed," Mr. Bucks said looking at the treasure pot "But where is the first pot? This is the one that was stolen yesterday."

"We are trying our best to find that as well, Mr. Bucks," John said. Taking it as an opportunity to get to the point, he said, "We were wondering how come you didn't hear the men digging out your first pot of treasure, unlike yesterday."

"I don't know," their client replied "Sometimes I get a very deep sleep, often when I am very tired. That night might have been one of them."

"We were also puzzled by the fact that the thieves knew the exact location of the first pot unlike yesterday," Joe pointed out "Someone must have known that you owned a treasure, and above all, he must have come to know somehow, the exact location of the first pot as well."

Mr. Bucks appeared to be lost in thought for a moment. Then suddenly his face brightened.

"How could I forget the most important thing that I noticed yesterday," he said suddenly remembering something.

"What is it, Mr. Bucks?" Jeff asked eager to know the reason behind their client's sudden excitement.

"I will tell you a story I hadn't told you before," Mr. Bucks said as he repositioned himself on the sofa "Remember Alexandru Lucas?"

"Yeah," John replied, "Your Great-great Grandfather's friend back in Romania from whom he inherited the treasure."

"Correct," Jean Bucks replied "Alexandru had a cousin back in Romania, the name I don't quite remember, who somehow had found out about the treasure. When he gave my Great-great Grandfather the treasure to safe keep, he had specifically told him to never hand over the pots to his cousin. They had some ongoing feud in the family and hence, they were not in good terms. However, money makes one blind, and his cousin did visit my Great-great Grandfather once after the war. He said Alexandru had sent him to retrieve the pots to which my Great-great Grandfather denied. However, after his death, one day when my Great Grandfather was away, a person visited my Grandfather claiming himself to be Alexandru's relative. The two soon got talking and my Grandfather even showed him one of the pots, the one towards the northern side of the backyard which was stolen on the first day. When the relative asked, my Grandfather even told him that the other pot was hidden towards the southern part of the backyard. He demanded my Grandfather to hand him back the treasure but my Grandfather made him wait till his father returned. When Great grandfather returned home, he found out that the person was no other than Alexandru's cousin's son. He chased him away and told my Grandfather the story about Alexandru's cousin which he wasn't aware of. A few months back, a man called, Darius Stefoniou, visited me and identified himself as Alexandru's Great-great Grandson. He looked to be in his early thirties and spoke with a Romanian accent. However, on researching a bit, I found out that Darius was actually the Great-great Grandson of Alexandru's cousin. I chased him away that day denying to hand over the treasure to him. Yesterday, when I went to the backyard to stop the men from stealing the second pot, I saw Darius there. He is the one who stole the treasure along with the other men, who must have been his friends, but I don't know where to find him."

"Wow!" John exclaimed, "We have got our main suspect then!"

11

Airborne

* * *

"I had forgotten to tell you guys about it," Mr. Bucks said quite sheepishly.

"It's ok, Mr. Bucks," Jeff replied still excited about what they had learned "This piece of information is going to help us a lot in solving this case."

"I hope so," Mr. Bucks said, "It's just that I don't know his address."

"We will find that as well," Joe replied quite confidently.

"You boys have been working hard and I am really happy that you got one of the pots back," Mr. Buck said smiling "I will make you a milkshake."

"That's cool, Mr. Bucks," John replied.

Jean Bucks went into the kitchen to prepare milkshakes for the boys. He soon returned holding a tray with four glasses of Vanilla milkshake on it. Presently, he handed one glass each to the three boys and took the last glass for himself.

"It's really good," Joe said complimenting Mr. Bucks.

"Thank you," their client replied, "It's a pity I don't have any chocolates at home, or I would have made you a chocolate milkshake."

"This isn't bad either," Jeff said.

"Yeah," John said, "It's really good."

"So how are you guys planning to proceed with the case now?" the client asked in his low tone voice getting into a more serious mood.

"We want to go back to the opening in the forest where we found the treasure," John replied, "Maybe we will find the first pot as well."

"Yeah," Jeff added "I know a pilot who flies a private helicopter to transport people. We will take his help."

"That's a plan," Mr. Bucks said quite satisfied "If you guys really find the first pot of treasure there, my happiness will have no bounds."

"We will try our best to get the pot back," Joe said confidently.

"Not only the pots," Jeff added "We will get the thieves as well for you."

The boys had started to like the big man by now. He seemed like a lonely man living alone in the big mansion all by himself. As the boys got more familiar with him, they learned that Jean Bucks was actually a quite cheerful man himself who loved company. He had friends at work, but they rarely visited him. So he tried to keep himself busy by learning gardening, playing the six strings and even cooking. He told the boys that even though the complete house was in such a bad state and repairs were overdue, he had no money for the same. The amount he earned from work was only enough to feed him and live a middle-class life. A house as big as this one would need quite a hefty amount of money for renovation. Even its maintenance demanded a lot of money which made Mr. Bucks neglect the house partially. He also told the boys that he couldn't afford to pay seventeen thousand and five hundred dollars to get back the treasure that was sold to the 24 Carat shop and so, he was hoping that the boys would soon retrieve the rest of the treasure before any more of it was sold.

The man even shared his personal life with the boys. He said that back in college in Philadelphia, he loved a girl named Tania Biller. Both of them were with each other and had decided to marry soon after they got a job. Work brought Mr. Bucks to Fischerberg City and took Tania to Huntsville. They were in contact for almost a year. They even met each other a couple of times but one day Mr. Bucks found out that she was cheating on him with one of her fellow workmates. That day, Jean Bucks decided that he won't marry anyone in his life as no one could be trusted. Not even the person he loved. He was left with only the family history and the ancient Romanian treasure which he had vowed to protect no matter what.

"We will get the treasure back for you, Mr. Bucks," Joe said, "You have our word."

"Thank you, boys," Jean Bucks replied, "I can't thank you enough."

"Here is a suggestion, though, Mr. Bucks," Jeff said, "You could use the treasure to renovate your house for once. You never know who will get the treasure after you and how he would use it."

"True," Joe agreed "For all we know, he might spend it all up and not give a damn about protecting it."

"This treasure was entrusted by Alexandru to us for safe keeping," Jean Bucks retorted, "I can't just spend it like that."

"But Alexandru is no more," Jeff said and then sensing that they might have offended their client, stated, "All we are saying is that even his family members have forgotten about the treasure, it seems. Instead, people from Alexandru's cousin's family keeps visiting you to take the treasure."

"You might have a point," Mr. Bucks said lost in thought.

"That was just a suggestion, Mr. Bucks," Joe said "We respect the loyalty your family has shown over the generations to Alexandru's treasure but I think you deserve to spend a small amount for your own betterment. It's not like you'd start to live a life of a king with it. You would just take a very small amount of the treasure for the house's maintenance and repairs. That amount won't be even significant to the total amount you have got in the two pots."

Mr. Bucks didn't reply anything and seemed to be lost in thought.

"I'm sorry if we offended you, Mr. Bucks," Jeff said breaking the silence after a few seconds.

"No, boys," the client replied "I am not offended. I was just thinking about what you guys said just now and it does make sense."

"Well anyway, we should be going now," John said getting up from the sofa "We will take your leave, Mr. Bucks."

"Sure. Do let me know if you find anything tomorrow."

"Without a doubt," Jeff said smiling.

"And thank you again for returning this," Mr. Bucks said smiling back as he held the pot of treasure "I will keep this in a safe place inside the house."

The boys bid goodbye to their client and soon got onto their respective bikes and went home wards.

The rest of the evening went quite uneventful. The boys updated their parents about the plan to go into the air to find the opening in the forest who wished them good luck in return. Jeff called up Mr. Hal Harper and asked him when he would be free the next day.

"I have to fly to New York in the morning. Meet me outside the airport in the afternoon. At around 12."

"Sure. Thanks a ton!"

Jeff called up John and notified him about the time. John downloaded a map of the area from the internet and took out its printout.

"This will help us mark the exact spot on the map," he told his younger brother.

"Good idea, brother," Joe replied.

They soon had dinner and lay down on the bed to call it a night.

"Mr. Bucks sure looks lonely," Joe said thinking about the man.

"He does," John replied amid closed eyes "All he has got is the treasure."

"Did you see how happy he was when he saw the second pot of treasure today?"

"Yeah, he was really excited."

"We got to get the first pot and return it to him," Joe said motivated.

"We will."

"Well, Goodnight!"

"Goodnight!"

Next morning, John woke up early and went to the gym. He loved to work out but he was too preoccupied with the case trying to find the stolen treasure and catch the thieves in the past few days. Since they had to go to the airport only in the afternoon, the boys were entitled to some free time in the morning and hence, John decided to visit the gym.

Joe woke up soon after and took a shower. Then he went downstairs to the kitchen cum dining room for breakfast. Oswald and Helena Martin were already there. Mrs. Martin was making Poached eggs while her husband was helping her prepare breakfast by making some orange juice.

"Good morning, Mom and Dad!" Joe wished.

His parents wished him back.

"Prepare your own corn flakes, son," Mrs. Martin said.

Joe went up to the kitchen counter and picked up a bowl and the box of corn flakes. Then he poured some flakes into the bowl and reached for the milk.

"Where's John?" Joe asked as the three sat down for breakfast with their bowls of corn flakes, poached egg, and orange juice.

"He went to the gym in the morning," his mother replied, "He should be back any moment now."

"So what are the plans for today?" Mr. Martin asked referring to the investigations.

"We are going into the air to find the exact location of the opening in the forest where we found the stolen second pot of treasure," Joe explained, "Then we will go back there and look for the first pot."

"I see," Mr. Martin said nodding his head in acknowledgment "But how are you going into the air?"

Joe told him and his mother about Hal Harper and how Jeff knew him.

Just then, the kitchen door opened and John walked in.

"Hi, everyone!" he greeted.

"Hello, John!" the others greeted back.

"I will go upstairs and freshen up," he said as he went out of the kitchen and into the hall.

As the three were just finishing their breakfast, the doorbell rang. Joe got up from his chair.

"I will see who it is," he said as he picked up his empty bowl of cereal and plate of poached egg and put them into the kitchen sink. Then he went towards the hall to open the front door.

"Hey, Jeff! What's up?" Joe asked as Jeff walked in from the front door.

"Hi, Joe!" Jeff replied "I thought we should plan out the trip and discuss the case before we left for the airport. We are anyway free in the morning."

"Seems legit," Joe replied closing the front door "Go upstairs. I will join you right away."

As Jeff went upstairs, Joe went to the kitchen and helped in doing the dishes. John got out of the bathroom and went downstairs for breakfast. The three assembled at John and Joe's room after about twenty minutes.

"I have got a map of the forest and its adjoining areas," John said showing Jeff the map he had printed out the previous day "This will help us mark the exact spot on it."

"Nice," Jeff replied "I was wondering how to go about in catching the thieves. We know the thief's name but where do we find him?"

"I don't know," Joe replied with a blank face "There are too many loose ends in this case to get an answer."

"We could start with the brown colored van, I guess," John suggested, "We didn't get its license plate number but we certainly can find it maybe?"

"But there could be numerous of those vans plying in Fischerberg City," Jeff replied not seeing much hope in John's idea.

"Yeah," Joe replied "But that van wasn't ordinary. While checking if there was someone inside it, I remember seeing the speedometer which wasn't an ordinary one. It was a modified dial with the word 'Flames' on it."

"And the right front door handle was colored silver. It was probably metallic," John pointed out remembering suddenly what he had seen that night.

"That gives us a way to identify the van," Jeff said

"But there will be a lot of those vans in Fischerberg City. We can't possibly track down all of them."

"I agree to that point," Joe said nodding his head.

"Yeah, it will be difficult to track them in this city," John said thinking "But not so difficult in Portville."

"Portville? Why?" Joe asked surprised.

"I have a hunch they have the hideout there. That opening in the forest was closer to Portville than to Fischerberg. Besides, it will be almost impossible to track the van down in this city but we could give it a try in Portville."

"Makes sense," Jeff said thinking about the idea "Portville is a small town. So we have a higher chance to trace out all the vans there."

"We can start off with the auto shops in Portville then," Joe suggested "If I am not wrong, Flames is a brand that makes modified parts for vehicles, like the speedometer, wheel covers, and vinyl. So we could go to the Flames dealers and ask them if they have any van in their records who got their speedometer changed."

"Not a bad idea," Jeff replied, "There won't be more than a few shops dealing in the Flames brand in Portville."

"But the problem is, why would the shops share their records with us?" John pointed out.

"I hadn't thought of that," Joe replied dejectedly.

"We will pose as project students doing a research or a study," Jeff said in reply to John's point "We will need a bonafide certificate from the Academy, though."

"I will ask Mr. Ice for the same," John said, "I am sure he will help us."

"Great, then," Joe said positively.

The boys talked about random things after that and soon, Jeff went home for lunch. They decided to meet at Jeff's house after an hour.

The three were off towards the airport after an hour. They started from Jeff's house and went east. They took the third right and onto the Johny Avenue in Adem Park and proceeded southwards. They reached North Austrot and took a left turn onto the Ring Road right after they crossed the District Library where Jeff's father worked. They crossed the South Central Park Football stadium on their way and soon took a right turn once they were in Urn Town onto the Airport Road. They parked their motorcycles at the private vehicle's parking and walked up to Luis Santos International Airport terminal. The terminal was buzzing with people, private cars, and taxis. A sniffer dog was doing his job right outside it with three security personnel in accompaniment. The five-lane road which had a designated bus lane opposite to the terminal building was crowded with all sorts of vehicles and a traffic policeman was having a hard time telling the drivers of the cars and taxis to hurry, who had come to drop or pick up people, in order to free up the parking lane for other vehicles.

Jeff noticed a tall and slim man who was in his forties waiting right outside the terminal gate 1 towards the west most part of the building. He was wearing a black racing jacket and trousers.

"There is Mr. Harper," Jeff told the others pointing towards the man.

The three walked up to the man and soon enough, the man spotted the boys approaching him.

"Hi, Mr. Harper!" Jeff greeted "These are my cousin brothers, John and Joe."

"Hello, guys," the man replied sporting a wide smile which seemed wider than his thin face.

"We are really thankful to you that you agreed to help us," John said.

"It's alright," Hal said "I know what you boys do and why you need my help. I will be more than happy to help you."

Mr. Harper led the way as the boys followed. They reached Gate no. 8, which was a private jet and helicopters only gate. Mr. Harper flashed his ID card to the security and told him that they were his friends who had wanted a ride on his chopper. The security personnel carried out a check on the boys and also checked their Identity Cards before letting them in. The four crossed the main lobby and got out of a small glass door towards their left. They could see the planes taking off and landing at the runway towards their right.

The airport consisted of two parallel runways to handle traffic during peak hours. All the gates for boarding and alighting were at the central area of the airport compound. The plane repairs and sheds were towards the western part of the premises whereas the eastern side was devoted to the private jets and choppers and the cargo planes with the cargo terminal located close by.

The three boys, led by Hal Harper walked towards the eastern side of the airport. Presently they reached a big shed which had a parking place for six choppers inside it, out of which four were occupied. The four walked in and stopped near an Airbus EC145. Mr. Harper unlocked the doors and told the boys to get in. The helicopter was a 9-seater with three seats on one row. John and Jeff occupied the first row whereas Joe got into the second row. Mr. Harper got into the pilot's seat and requested the Airport ground staff to pull the chopper out of the garage.

Soon, the three Js along with Hal Harper were ready to fly. Mr. Hal turned on the engine and the rotor started rotating, slowly at first but soon at full speed. After asking for clearance from the control tower, Mr. Harper made the chopper soon lift off the ground as it started to rise into the air. Once they were at around 4000 meters above the ground, they started to fly towards the Midlands Forest.

"Wow!" John exclaimed looking down from the window "The view is awesome from here."

"I can see the entire city from here," Jeff added.

"We will reach the forest in no time," Mr. Harper said.

The pilot took the chopper northwards and soon reached the Midlands Forest.

"Do you want me to land somewhere?" he asked.

"No, Mr. Harper," Jeff replied, "We just want to see the forest from up here."

"Oh ok," Mr. Harper replied.

The boys looked down at the forest from the air and noted any significant things that they could see on to the map John was holding.

"Could you get us a little more towards Portville?" Joe asked.

"Sure," Mr. Harper replied as he took the helicopter further north.

"There it is!" Jeff exclaimed over the noise of the chopper's engine "That's the opening, I guess."

"It indeed is," Joe said as he looked down.

"Look how big the opening is," John pointed out.

"It sure is," Mr. Harper said looking down himself "I wonder why there's an opening as large as that in the middle of the forest."

"We are trying to find out just that," Jeff replied.

Mr. Harper descended the chopper a little so that the boys could have a closer look at it.

"It looks like it is almost 20 meters in diameter," Joe noticed.

"True," Jeff agreed.

"I could land there if you want," Mr. Harper offered.

"No, Mr. Harper," John said, "It's fine."

With the help of Joe and Jeff, John marked the location onto the map. They stayed up for some more time noting anything important that they could see to help them find their way in the forest in case they were lost again.

"We are done," John said after about twenty minutes "You can take us back to the airport, Mr. Harper."

The pilot turned the helicopter south and started flying towards their starting point. They soon landed where they had started from.

"Thanks a lot, Mr. Harper," Jeff thanked the man as they got out of the chopper.

"You're welcome," Hal Harper replied, "Let me know if you guys want any more help."

They bid goodbye to Hal and got out of the airport. They soon reached the parking place where they had parked their bikes.

"It's still only 2 pm," Jeff said looking at his watch "How about we go into the forest to check the opening now?"

"Seems fine," Joe replied.

The boys got onto their bikes and sped off towards the Midlands Forest.

12

Trailing for a Trail

* * *

The boys took a right turn onto the Ring road which surrounded the entire city. Presently, they reached Downtown. They kept going north from there and after almost an hour, reached the highway that would take them to Portville. They stopped at a gardening shop right before getting onto the highway and rented three shovels and gloves. Then they got back onto their bikes and took the right turn onto the highway and traveled on it for about 15 minutes. Soon enough, John signaled the others to stop.

"We need to go in from here," John said as he got down from his bike.

"How far is it?" Joe asked.

"Seems like a fifteen to twenty minutes' walk," John replied.

"Let's get going then," Jeff said handing over one shovel to each of them.

The boys got off the highway and walked into the forest. They had merely walked for a few meters when they heard a loud sound which seemed to be coming from some kind of an engine.

"What's that sound?" Joe asked shocked.

"I have no idea," John replied equally surprised.

The three looked around to see if they could spot the source of the sound.

"Look there," Jeff said after a few moments pointing at the sky.

John and Joe looked up to see a helicopter flying close to the trees. It seemed to be coming from the direction of the forest and heading towards the highway. It flooded the air with its noise and birds flew away from the nearby trees chirping, their sound though, getting drowned in the noise of the engine.

"What is it doing here flying so low to the trees?" Jeff wondered out loud once the chopper had flown away and the noise of its engine and rotor had died down.

"It seemed to be taking off from somewhere," John replied.

"Or maybe landing," Joe added.

"Wait a minute," Jeff said his face suddenly brightening up.

"What's up, Jeff?" Joe asked.

"That makes complete sense," Jeff said sporting a grin on his face.

"What makes complete sense?" John asked confused at his cousin's sudden excitement.

"The chopper," Jeff started "was taking off. The opening in the forest that we are heading to. Remember Mr. Harper asked if we wanted him to land there?"

"So you mean," John said thinking along the lines of Jeff "that helicopter took off from there?"

Jeff nodded.

"That makes sense," John said "A large opening in the middle of the forest. What could possibly be its use other than act as a helipad?"

"But what was it doing there in that opening?" Joe

wondered.

"Maybe the thieves had come to retrieve the pot of treasure," Jeff replied.

"In that case, they must have found out that the pot is missing," Joe realized.

"Let's hurry over to the opening and see if we can spot anything before they return," John urged.

"Yeah, let's," Joe said, "But I still don't understand how a band of thieves can afford to have their own chopper."

"That implies that we are dealing with something bigger than just a bunch of thieves here," Jeff pointed out.

"Cut it for now," John urged again "Let's move quickly."

The three moved eastwards according to the map. The map John had got helped them immensely to reach the location of the opening without much problem.

"Here's the opening," John said.

"Let's look for any part of the soil that seems to have been dug out and filled in recently," Joe suggested.

"First, let's look around if there's anyone here," Jeff proposed.

The boys looked around for a while. They looked behind shrubs, bushes, and trees but got no sign of anyone being present there. After a few moments, they decided to go on with their operation. The three took up different corners of the opening and carefully checked the ground to see if it had any markings revealing that it was dug out recently. Digging out the whole area would be impossible for the boys and hence, they had decided on this plan.

The three Js started off at their corners and gradually cordoned off the entire area slowly moving towards the center. After two complete hours of checking the ground, the boys reached the center of the opening.

"Here are the tire marks of the chopper that took off a couple of hours ago," John said looking at a long and thick strip of an impression on the ground. There was no grass on this part of the opening.

"Here is the other tire," Joe called out from the opposite side.

"So we can safely assume that what Jeff said is indeed correct," John concluded.

"I safely assumed that I was correct long back," Jeff sulked.

"It's ok, Jeff," Joe said laughing "I was sure too."

"But we still didn't get any clues to the first pot of treasure," John pointed out.

"Maybe it's not hidden here at all," Joe quipped.

"Then we came on a wild goose chase," John said dejectedly.

"Hey," Jeff said looking offended "We wouldn't have got to know that this opening was serving as a helipad had we not come on this wild goose chase."

"Yeah, that's a positive," John said consoling his cousin amid a laughing Joe "I am sorry, Jeff."

The sun was starting to set and the three detectives decided to go home. The picked up their shovels and walked towards the western part of the opening. They were still a few meters away from the edge of the opening when suddenly they heard a buzzing sound. The boys stopped in their tracks and held their ground. At first, the boys thought it was the chopper returning but within moments, they realized that that was actually not the case. This sound was different to the one coming from the engine of the helicopter. Joe wanted to ask his brothers if they had any idea as to what the source of the sound could be, but before he could do so, he saw a horrifying sight.

One of the trees was tilting towards them and was gaining acceleration as it tilted further towards them. It seemed to come slowly at first, but then it gained speed as it came closer to the boys.

"Jump!" Joe shouted as he jumped out of the way, the tree falling down on the ground with a loud sound.

He got up from the ground to see if John and Jeff were safe and was delighted to see that it was indeed the case.

"How did that tree fall?" John said still shocked from the sudden danger.

"Hey, I think I saw movement there," Jeff said pointing towards the bushes and other trees from where the tree had fallen "I am going to see who it is."

Jeff darted off towards that direction.

"Be careful, Jeff," Joe called out as he jogged up to John "Don't go further into the forest."

"Are you alright?" Joe asked now looking at John.

"I am," John replied, "Give me a hand."

Joe helped John get back up on his feet.

"That was aimed straight at us," John said looking at the tree.

The tree wasn't so thick but it sure would have killed anyone who would have come under it.

"I am sure someone did this on purpose," Joe alleged.

The two walked up towards the edge of the opening and looked around for the base of the fallen tree.

"Here it is," John said, soon finding the base, "It sure was cut."

"Whoever did it surely wanted to kill us," Joe pointed out.

Just then Jeff emerged out of the forest and into the opening. He looked around for John and Joe. Sighting him, John and Joe went back to the opening.

"Saw anyone?" John asked.

"Yes," Jeff replied "There was a man. I gave him a chase but he went deeper into the forest. So I gave up."

It was starting to get dark and the boys decided to

stop their investigations here for the day and go home. They traced back the same route they had taken earlier and soon reached the highway.

"So what's the next step?" Joe asked.

"We go to Portville tomorrow to see if we can find the van," Jeff replied.

"Ok," John agreed "I will go to the academy in the morning to get the bonafide letter from my Professor. We will leave for Portville after lunch."

"Cool," the other two acknowledged.

The three got onto their bikes and rode off to their homes.

Next morning, soon after breakfast, John went to the academy to meet his Professor while Joe passed his time reading the unfinished novel that he had started to read the day Mr. Bucks had visited them for the first time regarding the case. However, he couldn't concentrate on it. His mind raced towards the case time and again and was diverted from reading the book. He wondered where the thieves' hideout could be. The boys had planned to try their luck in Portville but Joe knew it well enough, that there was a very less chance of actually finding the thieves there. He thought of the chopper that was operating from the open space in the middle of the forest. If the thieves owned a chopper, then they were in no way, just a small group. They had to be a part of a well-off thieves' faction. But how big was the faction and how dangerous were they? Joe didn't have the answer to that.

He also assumed that the first pot of treasure was hidden in the hideout of the thieves. But if that was indeed the case, then why did the thieves hide the second pot in the forest instead of the same location. Joe knew the key to all these questions was Darius Stefoniou, but where could they possibly find him. He wished he knew someone well enough in the Police Department who could help them with some information on the Romania. The boys sure had some contacts in the Police Department courtesy of the few cases they had solved so far but none of them the boys knew well enough, who could actually be trusted to keep quiet about the treasure. Mr. Bucks had made it clear that the cops shouldn't be involved in this case and that was indeed a setback to the boys.

Jeff, on the other hand, spent his time researching on the internet to find all the major auto shops who dealt with Flames modifications in cars in Portville. He got a list of six such shops and noted them down on a piece of paper with their address.

Soon, it was lunch time. John, who had returned with the letter by then, and Joe had a lunch of Quesadillas, Salad, and Yoghurt with their mother. At Jeff's home, he was having a meal of fish and chips with his mother. None of them had briefed their parents much about the happenings of the previous day, especially the falling tree, as it would make their parents more concerned. They decided to not concern their parents much unless it was really very necessary.

"I am going to Portville, Mom," Jeff said once he was done with the dishes after lunch.

"For the case?" Claudia Martin asked.

"Yeah."

"Ok, take care, dear."

Jeff got out of his house to see John and Joe reach the house on their bikes. He quickly went to the garage and took his motorcycle out.

"Let's go!" he said as he started the bike.

The boys followed the same route they had earlier followed to Mr. Bucks' house. They crossed his house and went further north on the highway. A few more minutes later, they saw the signboard saying 'Welcome to Portville'.

John signaled the others to stop and they soon

came to a halt.

"Where are the shops?" he asked Jeff.

Jeff took out the piece of paper from his pocket and showed it to the others.

"There are six shops," he said, "We can divide them among ourselves."

"Ok, first two are mine," Joe offered.

"Next two are mine then," John added.

"Cool, what do we have to ask for?" Jeff asked.

"For a brown van with a silver handle on the front right door," Joe replied, "The van has got a modified Flames speedometer."

The boys got back onto their bikes and rode off towards their respective shops. John had got three copies of the bonafide letter, one on each of the boys' names, which he had handed over to Joe and Jeff before starting off for their quest. They would have to say that they were students researching on how many vehicles carried out modifications.

After an hour or so, the three met at the same location where they had started from. They had decided to do so because Jeff didn't have a cell phone with him. Joe, who also had lost his phone back in the shed when he and Jeff were captured, was using John's old phone.

"Any output?" Joe asked with hope in his eyes "I got none."

"I got something from one of the shops," Jeff replied, "The person there said he had indeed carried out a speedometer modification on a van two weeks back, but didn't remember if it had a silver handle. I asked for his address, saying I was really fond of vans and just wanted to see it once. I know I sounded like some crazy creep, but well, it paid off and he gave me the address from his records."

"Great," John commented, "I got something as well. One of the shops said there was a van just last week who had come for a speedometer modification. The guy remembers well that it had a silver handle. He also said that the owner of the van paid only half the money. He had promised to return the next day with the rest of the money, and the store manager had agreed as a goodwill gesture. But it's been a week now and the van guy still hasn't paid the rest of the money, regardless of two notices from the store. I told the manager I had contacts in the Fischerberg Police Department and could help. So he gave me the address and told me to notify the van owner again. He also told me to warn him that he would report it to the police if he doesn't pay up within two days."

"Good for us that the van owner hadn't paid," Joe commented, "We got the address because of that."

"True that," John replied, "What is the address that you have, Jeff?"

"It's in Vinceton Park," Jeff replied.

"Mine's in Riverside," John said "Let's go to your location first. It's closer."

The boys took the main street that ran from the highway to the Port. They took the fourth right turn and reached Portville Police Department. The boys took a left from there and reached Vinceton Park which was solely a residential area with big mansions and exquisite villas. Vinceton Park was basically the posh area in Portville where all the rich people lived. The three Js reached the concerned house within minutes and parked their bikes on the side of the street.

"The van's there," Jeff muttered pointing at the driveway.

The boys looked towards the driveway and saw that the brown van was indeed there. A man was washing it with a jet spray. However, the van's back was facing the boys and hence, they couldn't get a clear look at the door handle of the vehicle to see if it was indeed silver.

"How do we manage to get a look at the handle?" John wondered out loud.

"Follow me," Joe replied an idea striking his head.

He led the way as the other two followed. The three went onto the driveway and Joe walked up to the man who was washing the van.

"Hi, there!" he greeted.

"Hello, who are you?" the man asked in a gruff voice looking puzzled. He looked to be in his forties and had a bald head accompanied by a big stomach. The man who was around 5'4" tall was sporting shorts and a beach t-shirt.

"I am Joe Martin," Joe replied, "Can you tell us how to reach Riverside?"

"Oh sure," the man replied "Go straight from here and take a left onto the Palm Street. Follow that till the street ends. At the last turn, take a right and you'll reach Riverside."

"Thank you very much, sir," Joe replied.

The other two had understood what Joe's plan was by now.

"That's a nice van, you have sir," John said as he walked around the van acting as if he was casually just looking at it.

"Thank you," the man replied with a smile.

The boys then took his leave and walked out of the compound of the house.

"What did you see?" Jeff asked once they were near their bikes.

"The van didn't have a silver handle," John replied.

"Oh, then that's not our van," Joe concluded.

"Let's go to Riverside then," Jeff said as he got onto his motorcycle.

The boys took the set of directions that the man had given them and soon reached Riverside. This area looked more like a middle-class area with a mixture of some run down houses, one-story bungalows, and a few four to five-floor apartments.

"This is the house," John said stopping a few minutes later in front of one of those one-story homes "House no. 21."

The three alighted their motorbikes and walked towards the driveway. They saw the van in the garage. The garage didn't have any door but again its back was turned towards the boys and hence they couldn't see if this one had a silver handle on its front right door.

"Let's walk in," Jeff suggested "There's no one outside in the compound. We will quietly go up and check."

John and Joe agreed and they proceeded onto the driveway as quietly as possible so as not to alert the occupants of the house. At the same time, however, they had to be careful so as to not arouse the suspicion of the passersby on the street outside and hence, had to look casual in their movement and not act like some thieves.

They reached the garage within moments and went towards the right side of the van. They looked at the door handle on the front right door.

It was silver!

However, before the boys could proceed any further, a stern voice called out loudly from behind,

"Hey! Who are you? Thieves!"

13

Spy on the Spy

* * *

The boys turned around startled and saw an averagely built man with a rectangular face looking sternly at them. He had blonde hair and looked to be towards his late thirties.

"Trying to steal my van, eh?" the man said, his face full of rage "I will show you what happens when you try to steal my van."

"What!" Jeff exclaimed "Thief? We? You are the thief. Where is your gang?"

He had decided that this man was indeed one of the thieves and this van was the one they were looking for because of the silver handle on the right front door. He closed his fist and got into an alert position in case of any eventualities.

"What gang are you talking about?" the man questioned even angrier now "Call me a thief, did you?"

"Yeah, I did," Jeff shot back. He felt someone grab his left arm. He turned to see who it was and saw Joe signaling him to cool down.

Joe then turned towards John and told him

something which Jeff couldn't hear. But he saw that John had widened his eyes in reaction.

"Look, mister," John said presently, "I think there has been a misunderstanding. We are from the Green's Auto Garage and the manager has sent us to notify you about the money you have to pay."

The man seemed to cool down a little at this.

"Ow! I told them I would pay," he scowled.

"It's been a week and the manager wants you to know that he will report a complaint at the Police Station if you don't pay within two days," John continued.

The boys saw the man forget his anger and lose his composure at the mention of the Police. But then he gathered his composure back a little.

"Wait!" he said frowning and looking straight at the boys "If you are indeed from Green's Auto Garage then what were you doing loitering near my van?"

"We weren't sure we had come to the right address," Joe replied making it all up, "Our boss said the van had a silver handle on the front right door and so we were just checking if we had come to the right place."

Jeff stood there looking puzzled. He didn't know what was happening. He was indeed clueless as to why his cousins had suddenly gone so soft on the man. The van had a silver handle and it was obvious to him that this man is a part of the gang of thieves who stole the treasure from Mr. Bucks' backyard. According to him, they should be pinning him down to the ground. The man, being alone, had no chance against the three boys.

"But your friend here called me a thief," he glowered.

"I am sorry," John replied in a consoling voice "He got angry because you called us thieves at first."

"Oh, ok then," the man seemed to cool down "I apologize. I thought you were thieves. Tell your boss I will pay him within two days."

The boys walked out of the compound and got onto their bikes.

"I don't understand what's happening," Jeff said looking lost as he started his bike.

"That wasn't our van, Jeff," Joe replied.

"But that had the silver handle we were looking for," Jeff argued.

"Yeah, but as you were engaged in the confrontation with the man, Joe managed to sneak a peek at the inside of the van and he saw that it wasn't the same speedometer we were looking for," John explained.

"Yeah," Joe agreed "It was a Flames speedometer, alright, but not the one I saw on the thieves' van the other night."

"Oh, well, ok then," Jeff said feeling quite embarrassed.

"What now?" Joe asked.

"Let's go home," John replied "It's almost four-thirty. We will stop by at Jean Bucks' place on the way to check on him. Later, we will go to our place and discuss what we should do next."

"Would he be available?" Jeff asked, "He might be off to work."

"Right," John replied "Let's hope he is at home."

"Cool then," Joe said, "Let's go."

"Wait, I will first go to Green's Auto Garage and inform him that the man said he will pay up in two days," John proposed.

"OK," the other two agreed.

The boys rode off on their bikes to Green's Auto Garage. John went into the garage as the other two stayed outside. The manager thanked John for his help and told him to come back if he wanted any more help regarding the project. Then the boys rode off towards the highway and went southwards on it towards Fischerberg City. They rode their bikes up the driveway of the huge mansion that belonged to their client and parked them there.

The boys walked up to the door and Jeff rang the doorbell. Within moments, the door opened.

"Hello, boys!" Jean Bucks greeted as he invited them to come in.

"How are you, Mr. Bucks?" John asked once they were seated in the hall.

"I am feeling quite well today," the client replied smiling "Thanks to you guys for returning the second pot."

"We just came to check on you," Jeff said, "Have you kept the pot of treasure safely somewhere?"

"Yes, I have. I have hidden it in the attic. So those men can't steal it again without coming inside the house and if they do come in, I will obviously get alert."

"That seems good," Joe accepted.

"So how's it going with finding the thieves and the other pot of treasure?" Mr. Bucks enquired with a face which showed signs of hope.

The boys briefed him about what they had done so far. They told him that they didn't find the other pot in the opening in Midlands Forest. They also told him about their search for the van in Portville.

"Oh, well," Mr. Bucks said looking a little disappointed that the boys hadn't made much of a breakthrough since returning one of the pots "Keep going. I am sure you'll find them."

"We are trying our best, Mr. Bucks," Joe replied reassuringly.

Just then, John noticed something moving at the window right across him. He looked at it from the side of his eyes still maintaining eye contact with their client. There was a figure peeping in through the window trying to overhear their conversations. John wanted to go after him chasing and try to catch him but then another idea struck him.

"Well, we should be leaving then, Mr. Bucks," he said suddenly, "We will resume our investigations again tomorrow."

"Oh ok," Mr. Bucks replied, "What are your guys planning to do next?"

"We haven't thought of that yet," John replied "We are too tired today. We three will decide what to do next tomorrow."

"But aren't we supposed to discuss the case today evening?" Joe asked turning to John with a puzzled expression. He wasn't aware of his elder brother's idea.

"Nah," John replied bringing out a fake yawn "I am too tired for today."

"Well, you guys get home and rest then," Mr. Bucks said as he led them towards the main door.

John caught a glance of the man standing at the window. Seeing the boys go to the main door with Jean Bucks, the man hurried off towards the front of the house. As Mr. Bucks opened the door, John looked around to see if he could spot the man. But the fugitive was nowhere around.

"What's up?" Jeff asked seeing John impatiently looking around for something.

Just then, John saw a scooter passing by the highway outside. It seemed to be accelerating and was headed towards Fischerberg.

"Come on," John said hurrying off towards their motorcycles "We got to follow that scooter."

"Why are we following him?" Joe asked as he got onto his bike. He was puzzled as much as Jeff by John's sudden excitement.

"He was trying to overhear our conversations," John replied.

That was all that Joe and Jeff needed to hear. They

started their motorcycles and rode out of the compound and onto the highway. They could see the scooter a few hundred meters ahead. He was unaware of the fact that the boys were behind him.

"We will follow him and see where he goes," Jeff suggested.

The boys stayed back a few hundred meters and maintained that distance. The scooter rode on unaware and took a right turn once he reached Fischerberg City and onto the Ring Road. John took the right turn and followed him while signaling the others to go straight. This was a surveillance strategy that the boys had seen in a movie. In this plan, only one guy followed the suspect at a time. The basic reason behind this is that the suspect may get suspicious if the same vehicle keeps following him for a long time. So the present follower maneuvers away from the suspect vehicle after some time and another following vehicle comes in to follow the concerned vehicle for some time. Soon, the second vehicle takes a different route from that of the suspect and another vehicle comes in into the picture. The plan required all the drivers engaged in the surveillance plan to be connected to each other via a wireless, but the boys had to make do with their cell phones. Since Jeff didn't have a phone with him, he and Joe were supposed to be acting as one unit while John alone was the other unit.

Presently, John followed the man on the scooter as he headed west. Joe called up John after a few moments.

"Where is he going to?" he asked.

"He is going west," John replied, "We are currently in North Central and about to reach Echo Park."

"Ok, I and Jeff will take it up from there," Joe offered.

Whenever the man stopped at a red signal, John made sure that there was a car or bus between them so that the suspect couldn't see him. John knew that the man, whoever he was, would certainly recognize him if he saw him even once, so he had to be very vigilant in order to not reveal his face.

They soon reached an intersection near the Echo Park. John looked around and saw Joe and Jeff's bikes on the road on to his left. The scooter driver had taken up the right lane and went straight without having to wait for the signal. John took the left lane himself and stopped at the red light. The green light flashed on the road where Joe and Jeff were on and they both resumed the surveillance taking the responsibility on from John.

This surveillance tactic was like a relay race where one runner ran at a time and passed the baton as soon as he reached his partner. The partner would start running then and would pass on the baton to the next teammate.

Since there were two bikes following the scooter now, Joe and Jeff had to be extra careful so as not to reveal themselves to the suspect. They followed the same plan John had followed earlier by making sure there was a car or bus between the boys and the scooter. They went on straight on the Ring Road and presently, crossed the New Heroes Memorial. Joe heard his phone ringing. He pulled it out of his pocket and saw John's name flashing on it.

"Where are you guys?" he asked.

"We just crossed the New Heroes Memorial," Joe replied.

"Ok, I am on the street that is to the immediate left of the Ring Road. I will take up the mission from the first intersection in Louisiana."

"That's assuming he goes straight."

"Right."

The intersection that John had talked about was the next upcoming intersection. Joe signaled at Jeff and both of them took the left lane. The scooter had once again taken the right most lane meaning he would travel straight once again. The green light was presently on and the boys took a left turn after the man on the scooter had gone straight to continue on the Ring Road. The boys crossed John on their way who was waiting at the red light.

Jeff signaled at John saying that the man had gone straight. John nodded in acknowledgment. Joe and Jeff took a right turn at the next intersection to head towards west. John had by now, gotten onto the Ring Road and was looking for the man.

After a few moments, Joe called up John to ask him where they were headed.

"I can't find him," John said upset "The red light made me lose a lot of time in continuing the chase."

"Oh no!" Joe replied dejectedly "Now what?"

"I am still looking for him. I hope I find him."

"Wait a minute!" Joe said suddenly signaling at Jeff at the same time "We can see the scooter."

"Are you sure it's him?" John asked.

"Yeah," Joe replied, "He's stopped at a house in By Lane no. 1."

"Where?"

"In Louisiana."

"Coming right up."

"He's going up onto the driveway of the house presently."

"Keep a watch on him. But don't go into the house. I will reach in a minute."

"Roger."

Joe and Jeff parked their bikes on the side of the lane and got down onto the footpath.

"There's John's bike," Jeff pointed out after a couple of minutes.

John came to a halt near the other two and got down himself onto the footpath.

"Which house did he go to?" he asked.

"The third house on the right from here," Jeff replied.

"What should we do now?" Joe asked not able to think of any ideas.

"I would have loved to have a look at the inside of his house," John said.

"But how?" Jeff pondered, "He is inside."

"That's the problem," John agreed.

"How about we first go up to the house to check if he lives alone or whether there are more people inside?" Joe proposed.

"Seems good," Jeff replied, "Besides, that house could be the hideout of the thieves as well."

The three boys walked up to the concerned house, which was a one-story bungalow and got onto the driveway. The house was medium sized with a small porch at the front and a small front yard. The house, however, seemed quite well off for a thief, which made the boys question themselves again about the financial status of the men they were dealing with. The thieves reportedly lived in middle-level houses like these and also owned a modified van. As if that was not enough, they even had a helicopter for themselves. If the thieves were so well off, then why did they get into this stealing business? Was it just for the sake of stealing or was it something more than that? Maybe something related to the Romanian family?

Presently, the boys walked up quietly to the side of the house and peeped in from one of the windows. They could see the hall from there but there was no one inside.

"Stay here, John," Joe said, "I will go and check the back."

"I will secure the front," Jeff claimed, "In case anyone walks in from the front yard."

Joe walked up towards the back of the house and

peeped in from one of the open windows at the back. He could see the kitchen from there. He spotted the man they had followed looking for something in the refrigerator. Then he suddenly closed the door of the fridge and walked towards the front of the house.

Joe hurried back towards John.

"He is coming towards the hall," he said.

"I can see him," John replied.

The fugitive, however, didn't stop at the hall. He walked on towards the main door of the house.

"Got to alert Jeff," John said rushing towards the front.

"Jeff, he is approaching the front," he whispered out once he was close enough to Jeff.

Jeff hid behind the side wall of the house just as the man emerged out of the main door and locked it behind him. Then he got onto his scooter, which was parked in the driveway and rode off.

"Where did he go?" Joe wondered getting out of hiding.

"Uh, he didn't tell me," Jeff replied quite sarcastically.

"No time to waste," John said getting back to the point "We need to somehow get into the house. There's no one else inside."

"Yeah, he locked the door as he left," Jeff agreed.

"There's an open window in the kitchen," Joe let the others know "We can get in from there."

"Let's hurry, then," John pressed.

The three went towards the back of the house with Joe in the lead and soon got in through the open window. They studied the plan of the house once they were in and identified two bedrooms, a hall, and the kitchen.

"I will take the hall," John said.

"I will go for the first bedroom, the one towards the front," Jeff said.

"That leaves the other bedroom for me, then," Joe concluded.

The three got into searching their respective rooms. John looked under the sofa, under the carpet, behind photos hung on the wall and even under a table lamp on one of the side tables. The hall looked quite well maintained and well decorated. Not only the hall though, the entire house was well maintained and decorated quite decently with appropriate furniture and show pieces which made the boys reiterate on their thought of how the thieves actually turned up to be thieves if they were indeed having such a good life.

Joe looked under the pillow, mattress, and the bed. Jeff did the same. They searched for anything that they could find which would tell them about the identity of the person or anything related to the thefts at Mr. Bucks' place.

Presently, Joe pulled out a drawer and found a file inside. He opened it and went through the documents in it

"Guys!" he called out as he walked into the hall with the file.

"What's up, Joe?" John asked walking up to him.

"I guess, I found out who this man is," Joe replied "His name is Adrian Clarke, an Australian by birth and works as a store manager at Starbucks in North Central. These are the house ownership papers."

"Cool," Jeff said, who had walked out of the bedroom upon hearing Joe call out to them, "That's his identity then. Now let's look for something that can help us with the case."

"Agreed," John replied and the three boys got back to their respective rooms to search.

As the three carried on with their search, John suddenly got an idea. He walked up to the telephone in the hall and opened its call log. He then took out his cell phone and noted down the recent incoming and outgoing call numbers. Just then, he heard a roaring sound outside and rushed towards one of the windows at the front to see what it was. He noticed that the man had returned on his scooter and was presently parking it on the driveway.

John rushed towards the bedrooms and warned Joe and Jeff about the man's return.

"But we didn't get anything related to the case," Jeff said gloomily.

"We will come back later," John replied.

The three rushed to the kitchen. John got out of the window first with Jeff behind him.

"Joe, what are you doing?" Jeff asked as he saw his cousin brother still standing in the kitchen. The boys could hear the front door being unlocked and there wasn't much time before the man would get into the house and notice Joe if he didn't hurry.

"I want to check one last place," Joe replied.

He walked up to the refrigerator and opened the door. He had seen the man, that is, Adrian Clarke looking for something in the refrigerator earlier after which, he had left the house. Joe hoped that maybe, just maybe, he could find something there. He knew there was almost zero chance and that if he didn't hurry, Adrian might notice him.

Still taking a huge risk, Joe opened the refrigerator door swiftly. He looked in but saw only vegetables and meat apart from some other stuff such as a loaf of bread, butter, and jam. Disappointed, he was about to close the door when something else struck him. He opened the freezer door and saw a piece of paper lying there. Joe heard the front door lock clicking and the knob getting turned. He quickly took the piece of paper and clicked a photo of it with his phone.

John and Jeff looked on anxiously and on the edge as Joe was on the verge of getting spotted. He quickly placed the piece of paper back in the freezer and closed the refrigerator door as quietly as possible. He could hear footsteps in the hall towards the front of the house. Joe dashed as quietly as possible to the open window and with the help of his brothers got out of the house just as the man entered the kitchen.

14
Decoded

* * *

The three Js quickly ducked below the window and quietly walked towards the side of the house and then towards the front. Soon, fully successful in their attempt to not get spotted, the three walked out of the compound and onto the street outside.

"What did you find?" Jeff inquired as they walked towards their motorbikes.

"A piece of paper," Joe replied, "I didn't have time to look at it but took a photo of it with my cell phone."

He took out his phone from his pocket and opened the image he had taken. The piece of paper showed a big red 'O' with a much smaller red 'x' in brackets beside it. Below the big 'O', there were the words in handwriting, 'Meet at 5 (x=12)'.

"What could this be?" John wondered.

"Looks like some sort of a message," Jeff replied looking at the image carefully and analyzing it.

"There is a meet, or was a meet, at 5, sure," Joe pointed out "But what is this x and o?"

"Looks like that's some sort of date, person or

address," Jeff replied intuitively. "Meet someone at 5, or at some address, or on a particular date."

"Seems to make sense," John replied.

"Let's get back to our home and figure this out," Joe advised.

The other two agreed, and were happy that they had actually found something in the house related to the case. They rode on towards home, feeling a sense of pride among themselves.

Mr. Oswald Martin, who had returned from work by now, opened the front door letting the boys in.

"You guys look like you are really tired," Oswald Martin said looking at the boys.

"We are," John replied, "We have been doing a lot of work today."

"What work?" his father asked.

The three boys updated Mr. Martin about their trip to Portville, following the eavesdropper and searching the house when the fugitive had gone out. They also told him about the note they had found.

"So we are going to our room now to figure out what the note is about," Joe concluded.

"That's a lot of action you guys have been getting," Mr. Martin said admiring the boys' skills at playing detective "Your mom will call you for dinner soon, though."

"That's ok, Dad," John said checking his watch "We still have an hour or so left."

The three Js went upstairs to the brothers' room and made themselves comfortable. John and Joe sat on their respective beds while Jeff took the computer chair for himself. He neatly made three copies of the exact image that Joe had taken and gave one note each to John and Joe. He kept the third note to himself. Looking at the image on the phone and analyzing it there was too much of an inconvenience and hence Jeff thought up of this idea and drew the image out on a piece of paper. He even used red ink to draw the small 'x' and big 'O'.

The boys looked at the image analyzing it from different directions wondering what it could be. They had come across numerous puzzles and codes like these and were quite good at cracking them. In this case, the message was quite clear, but the only thing that the three Js needed to crack was the 'x' and 'O'.

"No one will have a name with 'x', right?" Joe asked.

"Xavier?" John guessed shrugging "But I don't think 'x' is for a name. Maybe 'o' stands for a name."

"There will be plenty of names with 'o'," Jeff replied, "We won't be able to guess the name correctly just like that."

"I have an idea," John exclaimed as he suddenly took out his phone "I got the recent incoming and outgoing call numbers from the telephone back in the house. We can use True Caller to see who these numbers belong to. We might find someone's name starting with an 'x' or an 'o'."

"Brilliant," Joe lauded his elder brother.

Jeff switched on the computer and opened True Caller on the internet. John had noted down five numbers and he told them to Jeff one by one who typed them in the search bar.

The first number belonged to some Steve Clarke.

"Must be some relative of his," Joe predicted.

Jeff typed the second number and the search result said it belonged to a Rob Clinton. The boys had no idea who this was but noted down the name in any case. This person could be one of the gang members and might come in handy later on in the case.

Jeff typed the third number and the three boys' expressions changed to a shocked one as they read the name on the screen.

"Darius Stefoniou!" Jeff exclaimed.

"So Adrian is indeed with Darius in carrying out

the thefts," John concluded.

The fourth and fifth number belonged to a Stephen Carter and Vanessa Fryer respectively. The boys noted them down as well.

"So there are no names with 'o' or 'x,'" Jeff concluded.

"That means these do not stand for a name," John added.

"I guess 'x=12' is the key to this code," Joe said thinking hard.

The boys tried different techniques to crack the code with the key but in vain.

"Maybe this is not an 'o' at all," John guessed "Maybe it's a zero."

"In that case, the message turns out to be zero one two, because 'x' is equal to 12," Joe pointed out.

"But that again makes no sense," Jeff replied.

The boys kept trying for some more time before Mrs. Martin called them for dinner.

"Well, let's try again tomorrow, then," Joe suggested.

"Yeah," Jeff and John replied in unison.

Jeff bid goodbye to the Martins and soon was homebound. John and Joe went downstairs to the kitchen to have a dinner of sausage and potatoes and soup.

"How's the investigation going?" Mrs. Martin asked as the four sat for dinner.

"It's going pretty good," John replied, "We are presently trying to crack a code we found today."

"Did you find out how many men are there in total in the gang?"

"Not yet, Mom," Joe replied.

"They have done a lot of work today," Mr. Martin informed his wife and told her briefly about the boys' adventures that day.

"Nice," she replied once her husband was done with

the briefing "You guys must be getting close."

"Yes, we are," John replied confidently "We believe the code we got today will give us a huge breakthrough."

"Why didn't you catch the man you guys were following today?" the boys' father asked looking a bit confused "He is surely a part of the gang, right?"

"We could have caught him easily," Joe said "but had we done so, we wouldn't have known if he is indeed telling the truth. He could have given us fake answers and then we wouldn't have known how many men are actually there or even, where the other pot of treasure actually is."

"Yeah," John added "So we are trying to first find the hideout of the thieves. Once we do that, we will know how many men are actually there in the gang as well. Also, the other pot must be in the hideout. So we will get that as well."

"Good thinking," the parents' applauded.

After dinner, the two boys went to their bedroom and changed.

"You know what," Joe said, "I feel there's more to that opening in the forest than just hiding the treasure there."

"Yeah, that was also meant for landing a helicopter," John replied.

"But why do they need to land a chopper in the middle of the forest? Just to hide a treasure? Did they clear up that patch of land for the mere purpose of hiding the treasure? That too only one of the pots? Doesn't make much sense," Joe wondered.

"Beats me," John replied shrugging.

"I really think there's something else in there as well," Joe enforced.

Just then, John's cell phone rang. He picked it up from the nearby side table and saw it was Jeff.

"Hello, Jeff," he greeted.

"Any breakthrough on the code?" Jeff asked.

"Nah," John replied "We haven't tried cracking it since dinner. We thought we might get new ideas tomorrow."

"I see," Jeff said, "I can't get my mind off the code."

"There's more to the case than just the code, though. Joe was just pointing out that the opening in the forest being used just for the purpose of hiding the treasure doesn't make sense. They wouldn't land the helicopter just for that, right?"

"What was the shape of the opening?" Jeff asked with a sudden excitement in his voice.

"Kind of circular," John replied.

"That solves it then," Jeff quipped "I have cracked the code, I guess."

"Really?" John exclaimed, "How?"

"The code is probably a location. Whoever sent the message to Adrian told him to meet him at that particular location at five. So the 'o' is the big opening in the Midlands forest, and the x beside it is probably the exact location where they have to meet. That is, towards the eastern side of the opening."

John was stunned by Jeff's explanation. It made complete sense. Joe was just pointing it out that the opening had more to it than just a helipad or a location to hide the treasure, and now it actually seemed like the opening certainly had more to it. But then John recalled something.

"Wait, Jeff," he said cutting short Jeff's excitement "What you said makes a lot of sense. But you forgot that the note also mentions that 'x' is equal to twelve. So what does that stand for?"

"Oh," Jeff said depressed "I had completely forgotten about that."

"But I think I have it," John said after pondering over it for a few moments. It was his turn to get excited.

"You solved it?" Jeff asked from the other end.

"Yeah. The 'x' beside the 'o' doesn't indicate that they have to meet towards the east of the opening. It means, they have to meet at 'x', and 'x' is equal to twelve. And on a clock, twelve is towards the north…"

"So that means the northern side of the opening!" Jeff completed the sentence for John "We have solved it!"

"But is it five in the morning or evening?" John pondered.

"I don't care," Jeff replied "Let's go to the location tomorrow and check. I believe we will find the hideout there."

"Probably," John agreed "Let's go at four in the morning. That way, we will have a chance to see if the meeting is indeed at five in the morning tomorrow."

John put down his phone and looked happily at Joe. Joe, who had no hint of what was happening and was completely puzzled at the beginning of the conversation, had gathered some idea from what John was speaking on to the phone.

"We have cracked the code," John admitted to his younger brother.

"I guessed it," Joe replied, "But how?"

John told him how he and Jeff had deciphered the code.

"That's amazing!" Joe exclaimed, "So we leave at four tomorrow."

The boys quickly tried to catch some sleep. They had to wake up at around 3 30 in the morning if they wanted to go to the forest at four.

"That was quite impressive, Jeff," Joe lauded his cousin on cracking the code as the three rode towards the forest.

It was ten minutes past four and the boys were on their way to the Midlands Forest. The roads were empty and the city was still sleeping. There was a cold mist in the air which had forced the boys to wear their jackets. Visibility was a little low but the boys didn't have much difficulty with the head lights on. They knew, though, that they would have a hard time in the forest because there would be even more fog there at this time, unlike the time when John and Joe had lost their way.

They rode eastwards on the Ring Road. They soon crossed the Echo Park and after two intersections turned left onto the Fischerberg City - Portville Highway which went through the Midlands Forest. John had brought the map they had made, along with him. The boys decided that they would park their bikes in such a location so that they have to walk straight eastwards to reach the opening. They would then move north in search of the meeting point, which the boys had assumed would be the hideout of the thieves.

As they rode on the highway, they soon spotted a brown van parked on the right side of the road. The three boys came to a halt and got down on their feet.

"This is the same van," Joe identified looking at the silver door handle on the right side front door and also looking inside to see the speedometer.

"That proves that the meeting is indeed at five in the morning," Jeff established.

The boys got back onto their bikes and went forward towards their designated location of parking the motorcycles. They reached the location after a few minutes.

"Let's move east now," John said as he got off from the road and entered the forest.

"Be careful," Joe instructed, "There may be gang members roaming around as well. Remember, someone tried to kill us with a tree."

"Yeah," the other two replied in unison in agreement.

There was a lot more fog than the boys had expected and it made things a lot more difficult for them. Their sight was reduced drastically and as they progressed further into the forest, things just became more and more challenging. They wanted to switch on the flashlights of their phones, but they resisted themselves as that might just warn the thieves if they were anywhere close by. Fighting the cold breeze and fog, the boys kept hiking eastwards, their walking pace slowed down by the low visibility. The three Js evaded dangling branches and thorny shrubs and kept walking.

Soon, they reached the opening and the sight imparted more excitement into the boys.

"The chopper is here as well!" Jeff exclaimed in a whisper as he saw the large black machine looking at them through the white fog. Its rotor blades seemed to stab the mist as it hung down from the motor. The black color gleamed in the little moonlight that had managed to reach it in spite of the heavy fog.

"The meeting is surely on," John said.

The boys looked around to see if they could spot anyone in the opening but didn't see anyone. They couldn't make out if someone was indeed there towards the far side of the opening for there was too much fog to see that far. They decided to carry on with their operation and turned left and started moving towards the north. The boys had decided that they wouldn't walk into the opening for their own safety as someone might spot them. So they walked around the opening till they reached the other side and then started to walk north.

They kept walking for a few minutes. They had no idea how far the meeting place was. They just knew that it was somewhere in the north, but how far? The three merely had to keep walking until they found any evidence of the men present. It was almost five by now but the fog had still not ceded. As they went further towards the north, the boys started to take their steps really carefully so as not to place their footing on branches in the forest floor which would make a sound and could alert the thieves. They had a feeling that finally, they were extremely close to solving this case and finding the men and hence, didn't want to ruin this chance.

Soon, the boys came upon some trampled grass which seemed to make a trail towards the north.

"The men from the chopper must have followed this path," Joe inferred.

They followed the exact path and within a few moments came upon a cabin in the woods. Square in shape, it was one made with logs and was no bigger than about eight meters on either side. It had a door, which was trailed by a wooden board which was further trailed by two stairs made with wooden planks, on one of the sides and a window on the side facing the boys. However, the boys couldn't make out if anyone was standing at the window inside.

"This is surely the meeting place and the hideout," whispered Jeff.

15
Fight Cabin

❄ ❄ ❄

The three looked around the house to see if there was anyone outside. The fog made it difficult for the boys but soon enough, they were sure that there was no one at least on the near side of the house. They didn't have any idea as to whether there was anyone on the other side, though.

They tiptoed up to the window of the house as quietly and cautiously as they could. They could see four men talking inside, one of them being Adrian Clarke. Another man was short and bald and was sporting a sunglass even inside the cabin, that too when there were only fog and no sun all around. The three had the urge to giggle but they somehow resisted themselves. With the expensive-looking black boots the man was wearing, he seemed pretty rich in comparison to the other three.

Another one of them had a long face with his hair tied behind in a ponytail. He was about 5'11" and also sported a goatee on his face. From his actions, he seemed to be the one in charge of everything around, as he was constantly making gestures with his hands seeming to give instructions. The last man had a square face and was quite averagely built. He too was around 5'11" or 5'10" and had a scorpion tattoo on his neck.

The cabin had some chairs, table, a radio set on one side, and a few boxes lying around. Joe also spotted some ropes, a chainsaw, and a few jerry cans on the floor. The three tried to overhear what the men were saying but they were speaking in an extremely low voice much to the boys' despair. Joe gestured the others to follow him and the three got back into the forest away from the small cabin.

"We can't go in right now, there are four men," Joe pointed out.

"Correct," John agreed "We don't even know if they have weapons or not."

"I don't think they have any weapons," Jeff said assertively "We didn't find any when we searched Adrian's place."

"But we don't know about the others," John insisted, "Let's not take a risk."

"This is the hideout, alright," Joe decided "We just need an opportunity to get them."

"But are there only four or more than that?" John questioned.

That was something the boys weren't sure of and it made them feel uncertain of what to do next.

"Let's stay in the hiding and keep a watch on the cabin," Jeff suggested, "We may spot more people going in if there are indeed more of them."

"Seems legit," the other two nodded in agreement.

The boys took their positions behind trees and shrubs and crouched behind them waiting for something to happen. Minutes ticked by but neither did anyone go in nor did anyone come out. As the day started to break, the fog started to clear out and the boys' visibility was enhanced. Within a few more minutes, the mist cleared out considerably and the boys could see around the house more clearly.

"There's indeed no one around outside the cabin," Jeff concluded whispering at the boys.

Around forty minutes had passed but nothing had happened. Suddenly though, the door of the cabin flashed open. The three got into an alert position. They saw two men, one of them the rich guy in goggles, and the other, the square-faced tattoo guy, come out of the house. It meant Adrian Clarke was still inside. The boys though didn't have any clue as to which one of the other three men was Darius Stefoniou. The two walked on the board and then down the stairs. Then they marched towards the boys.

The three were alarmed and they carefully trod their steps and spread out moving away from the approaching men. John signaled to pounce upon the men when they approached but Joe denied and beckoned to stay put. The men went past the previous hiding location of the boys and walked southwards towards the opening. They didn't spot the boys neither did they hear anything.

Once the men were out of sight, the three boys came back to their original position.

"We could have easily overpowered them," John stated to Joe.

"We could have," Joe said agreeing to that fact but then countered John's idea "But what would we do after that? We have nothing to tie them up with."

"I agree with Joe," Jeff spoke up "Besides, had they just shouted out, the other two from the cabin would have heard them and would have rushed out and things would have gotten a lot more difficult for us."

John realized that his brothers were indeed correct. The boys would have just got into a big trouble had they agreed to John's gesture to ambush the two men.

"We can go into the cabin and take care of the other

two, though" Joe proposed.

"What if the other two come back?" John doubted.

"Doesn't seem like they would return anytime soon," Joe replied.

"Let's quickly go in and get those two inside," Jeff urged.

"Yeah, I also saw some ropes lying on the cabin floor," Joe stated, "We can use them to tie the men up."

"Yeah, I saw them too," Jeff added.

The three brothers quietly walked up to the cabin and stepped on the stairs and then walked on to the board. The old planks of the board sent out a creaking sound. The boys knew the men were alerted by the sound, but they couldn't do anything about it. They hoped that the men would think that their partners had returned. At the signal of Jeff, the three rushed towards the door of the cabin, the board sending out loud creaking sounds at every step that the boys made. It also made a thumping sound every time the shoes hit the board.

They reached the door of the cabin and barged inside. The two men were shock-stricken and before they could react to what was happening, John had gone over to Adrian and punched him in the face hard, making him fall down on the floor on his back. Joe and Jeff went over to the ponytail guy and grappled him. Jeff hit an elbow out on the man's stomach. The man leaned forward in pain holding his stomach with both hands but got a hard punch to the face from Joe in return. Adrian, out from the initial shock, got up onto his feet and tried to land a fist at John who dodged, moved behind the man and trapped his hands behind his back. The goon, not one to easily give up, bent his right foot and kicked at John behind him on his thigh. It was painful, but John didn't loosen his grip from the hands of the man.

On the other side of the room, the ponytail guy too had recovered from the initial surprise, and now he caught

Joe by his neck trying to choke him. Jeff landed a heavy fist at the man's right side of the head which made him lose the grip on Joe. Joe, released from the choking, grabbed his own neck with his right hand and coughed, amid trying to get fresh air into his lungs. The man, who had received the blow on his head sighted stars around him as he went through a temporary concussion. Jeff took this chance to get behind the man and grabbed his wrists against his back. He then forced the man to kneel down and placed his left hand on the man's head forcing him to look down.

Joe recovering from the choke realized that both John, who had forced Adrian into a similar stance as Jeff had done with the ponytail guy, and Jeff had gotten the two under their control. He reached for the ropes lying on the floor and found that there were only two ropes available. However, each of them was long enough to tie up two men. He took one of the ropes and went to John.

"Bring him over here, Jeff," Joe called out as Jeff obeyed.

Soon the two men were firmly tied up against their backs, the same rope around them. The boys relaxed for a moment.

"So, you are Adrian Clarke," John said looking at the man who was shocked by the fact that they knew his name.

"How did you know?" he asked.

"We will tell you later," Joe replied "Right now, it's our turn to ask the questions. Who are you?" he asked turning to the ponytail guy.

"Why should I tell you?" he said glaring at the boys.

The boys detected the Eastern European accent of the man and smiled at themselves. They were amused at the fact that he had given his identity away.

"So you are Darius Stefoniou," Jeff quipped.

The man looked at the boys shocked and cursing

himself that he had given it away.

"Look there's no point in keeping quiet," Joe said "We know who you are. So you better confess everything."

"Right," John said, "Why has your family been after Jean Bucks' treasure so much for generations now?"

Darius kept quiet. He didn't want to speak. Instead, he looked at the boys angrily.

"Speak or don't speak, all we want is the treasure back. So it wouldn't make a difference if you didn't cooperate with us," Jeff said shrugging.

The two still kept silent.

Just then, there was a thumping sound from the board outside followed by a creaking sound.

"The other two must have returned," Joe guessed.

"I will stay here to see that these two don't get themselves into any tricks," John proposed "You two take care of them."

John put one palm on the mouth of Darius and Adrian each and pressed so as to gag them. He didn't want them to alert their compatriots. Joe and Jeff went up to the door and stood against the wall on either side. The sound of thumping and the board creaking drew closer. The boys could make out that there were two men approaching. John, Joe and Jeff's heart raced like a horse as the sounds drew closer and closer. Suddenly, the door opened, and as the men walked in, they saw John crouched beside the tied up Darius and Adrian, who were seated on the floor, gagging them.

"Who are you?" the short bald headed man asked looking fiercely at John. He was still wearing the goggles and presently, his right hand reached for something behind his waist.

Joe caught a glance of what he was trying to reach for and it terrified him. There was a handgun tucked safely behind the short man's back. He knew that the game would be over if the man drew out his weapon. Hence, losing no time Joe jumped upon the man forcing him off his feet and falling down onto the ground. Getting the cue, Jeff closed the cabin door and before the square-faced guy could react, landed an uppercut with his fist on the man's chin. The man winced in pain. Jeff punched him in the stomach and followed it by a sweeping tackle with his legs which forced the man to fall down heavily on the floor releasing air through his mouth. The floor of the cabin sent out a loud thumping sound and it creaked. Jeff got on top of the man as John brought the other rope to help Jeff tie him up.

In the meantime, Joe had managed to pull out the gun from the back of the bald headed guy's waist and threw it out of the window breaking the glass as it flew by. Then he rolled the man over on his back and jumped at him. Seating on his chest, he punched the man's face twice. The guy had no energy to fight back. Joe rolled him back on his stomach and trapped his hands behind his back as he waited for John to bring the rope.

16

All That Glitters is Indeed Gold

* * *

Soon the two were tied up as well beside Darius and Adrian.

"So, it's confession time," Joe said looking at the four men with a grin.

The four realized that they were caught and had no chance to escape now.

Adrian spoke up at first.

"I am Adrian Clarke," he said, "But I don't know how you figured that out already."

"And we believe you work at the Starbucks in Louisiana?" Jeff supposed smiling.

Adrian was even more shock-stricken.

"How on earth did you find out?" he asked surprised.

"Well, remember yesterday you were spying on us at Mr. Bucks' place?" John asked, "We felt we should return the favor by spying on you."

The man's face went red as he realized how foolish and careless he had been.

Jeff, who was searching the man's pockets and wallets for their identity or any possible weapons that they might be having, got up onto his feet.

"Adrian is the one who had been spying on us forever," he said, "I found two Sweet-o toffees in his pockets."

"You love them, don't you?" Joe smirked and then turned to Jeff "Who are the other two?"

"The man in goggles is Winston Burns and the tattooed guy is Stephen Carter," Jeff replied looking at the identity cards that he had retrieved from their wallets.

"So Winston, you look pretty rich," John asked.

"He owns a casino in Las Vegas," Adrian replied and got an angry glance from Winston for revealing his identity. The boys were not sure though if it was indeed an angry glance. His eyes, covered by the sunglass, were not at all visible. They presumed however from his frowned face, that it was indeed an angry look.

"What?" he shot back at Winston "They have found out all about me and I am going to tell them all about you guys. I told you I wasn't good at spying but Darius and Stephen were too lazy to take the responsibility upon themselves. Look what that has got us into now."

Winston gave an I-don't-care look at his compatriot.

"Stephen works as a delivery guy for a company," Adrian said.

"So that's how you got the van," Joe inferred.

The four men nodded.

"Well, Darius, you still haven't answered our question," Jeff said looking at him "Why has your family always been chasing Mr. Bucks' treasure?"

"It doesn't belong to him," he replied in his Romanian-English accent "It belongs to Alexandru Lucas."

"We know that story," John shot back "We also

know that your ancestor, who was Alexandru's cousin, wasn't in good terms with him. So he had told Mr. Bucks' Great-great Grandfather to never hand over the treasure to him."

"But family comes before friends," Darius quipped amid a disgusted look "My Great-great Grandfather had lost his job an' the war had made it even more difficult to get one. We wer' in a very bad condition and wanted someone to help us with som' money. We couldn't even afford our two day's meals. My Great-great Grandfather found out somehow that his cousin had two pots of treasur'. He went to his hom' begging for help, but he denied helping him because of the ongoing feud. This enraged my Great-great Grandfather and he got into an argument with Alexandru. The argument soon turned into a fight and my ancestor ended up killing Alexandru. Horrified by what he had done, he ran out of the house. Alexandru's wife soon committed suicide when she found out that her husband had been killed. But we wer' not done. We still felt humiliated by how Alexandru had rejected my ancestor's begging and resolved that we would one day take the treasure for ourselves."

"Such heartless people your whole family is," Jeff said shaking his head with a pitiful expression.

"But why were you guys spying on us time and again?" John asked, "How did you people even come to know that Mr. Bucks had come to us for help."

"I found that out," Adrian replied with a proud expression on his face because of his personal achievement "I was riding on my scooter in Yorkville when I saw Mr. Bucks walking. He was coming from the direction of your house. I had heard about the three of you and guessed he must have gone to your place for help. So just to be sure, I went to your house and tried to overhear your conversations. My doubts were soon confirmed. I called up Darius and told him about it. He told me to keep spying on you three.

I told him I wasn't good at it but he still forced me to do it."

He wanted to glance a disgusted look at Darius, but he couldn't for he was tied up against Darius' back.

"Who threw the stone at my house?" Jeff asked suddenly remembering the incident.

"That was me," Stephen replied with a grin "You know, I have quite a good aim. Too bad, the rock didn't hit your mother though."

Jeff was enraged with Stephen's statement. He walked up to him and gave him a hard slap on his face with the back of his palm.

"Too bad, my hand didn't miss you," he said mocking him.

"But how did you three get into this?" Joe asked, "I mean Darius had a motive, but what about you three? Why did you join him?"

"For the treasure of course," Adrian replied, "That was a lot of money and Darius said ten percent of the treasure would go to each one of us three. Even that much percentage amounts to billions of dollars."

"So you guys knew Darius?" John asked.

"Darius was a friend of mine," Adrian confessed "We met after he came to Fischerberg City. I knew Stephen because he once lived in my neighborhood. I knew he loved earning easy money and hence, took him into the plan."

"What about Winston Burns?" Jeff asked.

"Winston is a rich businessman in Las Vegas," Stephen replied "He owns a casino, as Adrian had already told you. However, his business had been going down and was suffering huge losses. He wanted to make some reforms and wanted money for the same, but banks denied giving him a loan. I along with Darius and Adrian was discussing the plan of stealing the treasure in this cabin one day when suddenly Winston emerged from nowhere. He loves trekking and unfortunately, was trekking in these forests that day. He came upon this cabin and overheard our plans. So we had to take him in."

"I had contacts all over the place and could help them with selling the treasure at a good price," Winston who had been rather quiet till now, spoke up "Apart from that, I also had a gun and hence, could help them at times of trouble."

"Well, you wer' of no use today when we wer' in trouble," Darius shot back.

"So that chopper belongs to you?" Joe asked.

"Yes," the bald man replied.

"Who flies that?" Jeff asked wondering "Don't you have a pilot?"

"I have a flying license."

"So you guys cleared out the forest to make a helipad for him?" John asked.

"Yes," Adrian replied giving a sickening look at Winston "Apparently, he didn't want to travel to Fischerberg in a flight as that would make people suspicious as to why suddenly, he has been coming here so frequently. So he told us to clear a patch of land in the forest for his chopper to land."

"And where did you guys go now?" Joe asked looking at Winston and Stephen.

"Winston didn't believe that the pot of treasure had been stolen from the opening in the forest," Stephen admitted, "So I took him there so that he could check himself."

"But we saw his chopper leaving the forest when we came here after we had taken the treasure out," Jeff said puzzled "That was two days back. Didn't he realize the pot wasn't there then?"

"We ourselves hadn't checked on the pot," Adrian replied, "We did so only yesterday and found out that the pot wasn't there. We suspected that you guys must have found it somehow and taken it. That's why I went to Jean Bucks' place to spy."

"And where did you go yesterday after you returned from his place?" John asked.

"Yeah," Joe said, "You left for somewhere right after you returned home."

"I just went out to a nearby store to get some groceries."

"Was it you who cut down the tree near the opening trying to get us beneath it?" John asked still looking at Adrian.

"That was me," Stephen replied "After Winston flew away in the chopper, I was lazily coming towards this cabin after exploring around the opening for some time to meet up Darius and Adrian when I heard you guys approaching. I hid behind a tree and watched on as you three were checking for something in the opening. Figuring that this was a good chance to get you three out of the way, I came rushing here, took the chainsaw and reached the opening just as you guys were planning to leave. Wasting no time, I cut down the tree."

"You almost had us there," Jeff confessed.

"Another thing," Joe said remembering something suddenly "I remember you had walked in into the 24 Carat store, Adrian, but then you ran out after you noticed us. We were chasing you but then how did you hit us?"

Adrian smirked feeling a sense of pride yet once again.

"I ran into the alley and found a wooden rod lying on the ground. As I was picking it up, I saw an open back door of one of the stores. I went in there with the rod. When you guys reached the alley and were looking for me, I crept out behind you and hit you two on the head. Then I called Stephen who said he was close by, delivering a few things. He came up and we loaded you into the back of the van and took you to the shed."

"And you wanted us dead," Jeff fathomed which was almost certain according to the boys "So you guys broke open the knob of the cylinder to make it look like an accident."

"You're very smart," Stephen replied "We didn't expect to find the cylinder there. We just wanted to keep you there so that you two would be away from us until we had sold the whole of the treasure. I knew that no one lived in that house and that it had a shed at its back. But once there, we spotted the cylinder and thought we should do away with you guys for once and for all."

"But you two escaped," Adrian added gritting his teeth.

"Coming to the main question, though," John said, "Where is the first pot of treasure that you stole?"

"We won't tell you that," Darius replied with a smirk, "If you are so smart, find it yourself."

The boys got about searching the cabin. They looked for the treasure in the empty boxes, in the jerry cans, under the tables and everywhere else. They even carefully checked the ground and the walls in case there was a secret room somewhere, but came up with no results.

The four men were sneering at the boys.

"Where could have they hidden the pot?" John wondered.

"I think I know where it is," Joe replied excitedly after appearing to ponder over it for some time.

"Where?" Jeff asked.

"First let's call Mr. Bucks and show him these goons," Joe replied.

He went out of the cabin and into the woods in search of a mobile signal. He wouldn't get any signal inside the forest and hence would have to go towards the exterior part of the forest to get any mobile network. John and Jeff stayed behind in the cabin to keep a watch on the four thieves they had captured.

After about an hour, Joe walked in with Jean Bucks behind him.

"Hello, Mr. Bucks," John and Jeff greeted their client.

"Hello, boys!" he replied, "Such a great way to start the day!"

Just then, much to their astonishment, John and Jeff saw three policemen come in and this surprised everyone except Jean Bucks and Joe.

"Police?" Jeff exclaimed.

"I brought them along," Mr. Bucks replied.

"But…you didn't want any Police,in this case, Mr. Bucks," John said baffled.

"Yes," he replied "But yesterday night as I tried to sleep, I brooded over everything that has been happening. I have no children to look after this treasure once I am gone. Who knows, who will get their hands on it and for what purpose they will use it then. This worried me. I understood that Alexandru's family is never coming here to take the treasure back. They must have forgotten about it. So I thought, the best option is to hand it all over to the Government. But I have also decided that I will request the Government to send the two pots to the Romanian Government because it rightly belongs to them."

"Great thought, Mr. Bucks," Jeff replied impressed with his client.

"I was stumped as well at first," Joe said smiling "I was standing on the roadside waiting for Mr. Bucks but then I saw him coming over in a cop car with another patrol car behind it and this surprised me. Then he told me about his decision and I felt that was quite the correct thing to do."

"I told them about the case in the car," Mr. Bucks said.

"Did they confess everything, though?" one of the Police Officers with the name Frazer Campbell written on his nameplate asked. He was a huge African-American man with a bald head. Any culprit would be too scared to fight him, the boys thought. His fists looked big enough to cover the entire face of whomever he would punch. Any person in the world would love to stay free of trouble from this man, and thus the job of the Police rightly suited him.

"They have," John replied, "But I guess you'll need to record their statements."

"We will carry out the procedures at the Police Department," another officer named Alex Tenpenny said. This man was rather slim and shorter than Officer Campbell. He seemed to have aged and retirement looked quite evident. The wrinkles on his face spoke of the various brave acts he had put together during his career as an Officer. His gray hairs proved that the man was one of the most experienced Officers one could find.

The other police officer had the name Kipp Briar on his nameplate. He was rather young and seemed to be the most junior in ranks. He too was as slim as Officer Tenpenny but had a height taller than him. His face had the fresh excitement of joining the police force. Looking currently rather inexperienced though, he stood behind the other two Officers.

"But where is the other pot of treasure?" the boys' client asked.

"I will take you all to it," Joe replied amid a grin "Officers, you have got one more person to arrest."

"There's one more?" Jeff asked puzzled.

"Yes, brother," Joe replied still holding the grin "Follow me."

Joe led the others out of the house and into the forest. The four men under the firm custody of the Police Officers walked between the others. Joe led the way, followed by

John and Jeff. They were followed by Jean Bucks. The four thieves walked behind him followed by the three men in uniform. They presently walked south towards the opening. The sun had risen and there was no fog at all at the moment. The bright rays of the sun penetrated through the roof of the forest and reached them as they walked. Throughout the trip, John and Jeff kept asking Joe about who the fifth person was and where he thought the treasure was. Joe gave the same reply every time.

"You'll soon see for yourself."

Soon, they reached the opening.

"Officers, you'll have to take this chopper away I guess," John called out to the back.

"We will send out our men once we reach the department," Officer Campbell replied.

They took a right turn from the opening and headed west towards the highway. The crossed the dense cover of trees and bushes and after about fifteen minutes of walking reached the exit of the forest.

Joe got onto his motorcycle.

"Follow my lead," he called out as he started to ride towards Fischerberg City.

John and Jeff got onto their bikes and rode on after him. The Police who had come in two patrol cars stuffed the two of the thieves in each car. Mr. Bucks got into the first car with Officer Campbell and they started to follow the boys with Officer Tenpenny and Briar in the patrol car close behind.

Once they reached the entrance of Fischerberg City, Joe called out to Jeff.

"Take us to the 24 Carat shop, Jeff," he said.

"Why? Oh, you think he is involved?" Jeff asked confused.

"I will explain everything once we reach there," Joe replied over the sound of the bike's engine "Just take us there first."

Jeff still bewildered, started leading the way. He took a left turn onto the Ring Road and kept going straight on it. They crossed the Drake Police Station on the way but didn't stop there to turn in the culprits. After about forty-five minutes, they reached Downtown Fischerberg. Jeff took a right turn onto the Commercial Street 1 with the other following him close behind. At the next intersection, Jeff turned left onto Commercial Street 3. They reached the Downtown Circle and took the first exit on the right. They then turned onto the Heather way Street and soon, stopped in front of the specific store.

The shop had just opened it seemed. A staff from the shop was cleaning the front doors and the area outside. Joe and the others got down from their vehicles, except Officer Briar who was told to stay back to keep a watch on the men. Being junior to the other two, Officer Briar had to follow the orders even though he wanted to go into the store and watch the action.

Joe walked in with the others into the 24 Carat shop.

"Arrest this man, Officers," he said pointing at Dillon Johnson who was having his usual cup of coffee.

The two Police Officers got hold of the man.

"What?" Mr. Johnson exclaimed with surprise "What did I do?"

"You are in terms with the thieves who stole Mr. Bucks' treasure," Joe accused.

"No," the store manager replied grimacing, "You are insane."

"I will prove it," Joe replied with a smirk.

He went towards the back door of the store and went into the back room along with John, Jeff, Jean Bucks and Officer Tenpenny. Officer Campbell was still holding the man so that he couldn't run away.

Joe walked up to the desk and crouched beside it. He clearly remembered where Dillon Johnson's secret locker was. He removed the loose tile from its position and placed it aside. Then, much to everyone's astonishment, he pulled out the other pot of treasure from the pit.

"How did you know it was here?" Jeff asked amazed.

Joe explained about his encounter with the secret locker when he and Jeff had come to the store to catch the thieves. He told them how he had learned about the secret pit and that Mr. Johnson had kept the loot he had bought from the men there.

"The night the second pot was stolen, John and I were following the men in the forest. On walking up closer to them, we heard them mention the word 24 Carat. The men were talking about bringing the second pot here as well, and this made me suspicious because they had already found out by then that we knew they had sold a little part of the treasure from the first pot to Dillon Johnson. So they wouldn't have brought the treasure here after that because we had already alerted Mr. Johnson that what these men were selling was actually stolen loot, and the thieves knew that we had warned him. In spite of that, they wanted to bring the second pot to this store and sell it to Mr. Johnson. Today, when we searched the entire cabin in the forest for the treasure and couldn't find it, I got into thinking trying to realize where the thieves could have hidden it. Then I remembered about this secret pit here and everything fell into place. Dillon Johnson offered a very good price for the jewelry and gold and hence, the thieves didn't want to go to another store. Hence, they probably got Mr. Johnson into the plan with him. The manager must have been lured into it when he found out that the men had two pots of authentic Romanian treasure. He would gain a lot of profit by selling them to his contacts and so, couldn't turn down the offer."

"Brilliant!" Officer Tenpenny said, "That was

incredible thinking, Joe. You boys have really done a very good job."

The three boys and Mr. Bucks escorted the police and the thieves along with Mr. Johnson to the Police Department where they issued their statements amid being congratulated by the various Police Officers present there. Once the formalities were done, the boys along with Mr. Bucks walked out of the Department.

"I can't really thank you enough, boys," Mr. Bucks said with his usual husky voice. But it had cheerfulness in it that the boys hadn't seen in him so far.

"That was our job, Mr. Bucks," Jeff replied trying to look humble, hiding his enthusiasm "We are glad we could help."

"I will send you a cheque of ten thousand dollars tomorrow, nonetheless," Mr. Bucks said and then winking, he added, "Divide the treasure among yourselves."

"That kind of money is no less than a treasure for us, Mr. Bucks," John replied as the three boys gave a high five to each other.